NO GIG IS TOO SMALL

I0598284

ANDRE DUZA

deadite
press

DEADITE PRESS
P.O. BOX 10065
PORTLAND, OR 97296
www.DEADITEPRESS.com

AN ERASERHEAD PRESS COMPANY
www.ERASERHEADPRESS.com

ISBN: 978-1-62105-270-8

Jie Tsang '18

FEMA

Property of U.S. Department of Homeland Security — Mount Weather Emergency Operations Facility

The following documentary is property of the United States Department of Homeland Security in association with the Martin Stone Show. The film is presented uncensored and uncut, and contains profane language, explicit images, and acts of extreme violence. Some of the opinions expressed herein do not necessarily reflect the opinions of the U.S. Department of Homeland Security. Viewer discretion is advised.

A Serpentine Films Production in Association with the Martin Stone Show...

Video

A circular stage seemingly afloat in a sea of heads and shoulders. Hysterical feminine adulation directed toward the trio of lanky, androgynous rock stars power-posing at center stage. Pyrotechnics erupt behind the men. The crowd approves. Their cheers are deafening.

A montage of concert venues as a tour bus arrives. Fans waiting in parking lots. They run screaming alongside the bus.

Narrator (Voice-over): What started out as three friends passing the time at a local band camp, became one of the most influential rock bands of a generation. In the mid-to-late '80s nobody was bigger than Serpentine.

Concerts. Backstage. Champagne celebrations. Wet T-shirts. Fake tits. Serpentine at the number one spot on the Billboard Music Charts. Awards shows.

Narrator (V.O.): They filled stadiums and performed to sell-out crowds. They lived at the top of the charts and garnered award after award.

Drugs. Booze. Fast women. Drunken performances.

Narrator (V.O.): But a life of excess eventually took its toll on the trio and the band once named the most influential rock group in the last decade officially split up in 1991.

The group, older now, rocks out on a small, intimate stage in a packed nightclub. The crowd goes nuts.

Narrator (V.O.): Decades of hard feelings were put aside when the boys came together for a charity event in early 2014. Reaction from the crowd was overwhelmingly positive and it quickly became obvious that the time was right for a comeback. A documentary was planned to help kick off the return of Serpentine. The film would chronicle the daily lives of the bandmates while they worked on their new album.

An ambush of newspaper headlines dated 9/6/2014: THE DEAD WALK! Chaos in the streets. The breakdown of society via security camera footage from around the world.

Narrator (V.O.): But fate had other plans…

People fighting back against the dead. Landfills full of bodies. The evolution of settlements. The Martin Stone Show.

Narrator (V.O.): What started as a peek into the lives of three friends who became rock Gods, has evolved into a video diary chronicling humanity's struggle to survive, and Rock 'n' Roll's place in the resurrection of our once great society.

A title fades into view…

Episode #1:
Ride the Serpentine!

Video (Canon Vixia HF HD Camera)

May 17th, 9:32am
The interior of a modified van. All black. Plush, leather seating fit for a private jet in front. The rear seating has been removed, giving the illusion of space. A leather bench spans the length of one side. A console reminiscent of a news van embedded in the opposite wall. A small monitor in the center. A short counter below. Several boxes stacked against the back doors. A duo of guitar-cases rest against the boxes. Tinted windows dim the natural light. The Vixia perched atop a swiveling dashboard mount. We intercut between forward, side, and rear-facing views.

"Rock 'n' Roll Ain't Noise Pollution" by AC/DC wafts from the speakers.

A heavily inked, Viking of a man (Jules Yeager, 51) is seated on the bench. A living stick-figure with a face full of wisdom (James "Holly" Hollister, 50) behind the wheel. An effeminate, seemingly ageless pretty-boy with long, dark hair and sharp features (Graeme "Gramps" Gunz, 48) riding shotgun, and occasionally manipulating the Vixia.

Jules blindly fingers an acoustic guitar, his eyes glued to the blank monitor across from him. Graeme is equally focused on the scenery outside the passenger-side window.

Graeme: These back roads are all starting to look the same.

Hollister: Trees and farmland.

Graeme: ...and messages spray-painted on water towers.

Jules (V.O.): Welcome to the apocalypse of the apocalypse, folks! I'm your guide, Jules. You may remember me as the axeman and song-writer extraordinaire from the baddest band on the planet, Serpentine. And if you remember me, then you definitely remember that Skeletor-faced bag-a-bones at the helm, James "Holly" Hollister on drums, and to his right, the long, tall serpent himself, Graeme Gunz on bass and lead vocals. We call him Gramps. (Whispers) His real last name is Fischback.

Graeme: There're less of 'em out in the open.

Hollister: The trees…

Graeme leans closer to the window. His eyes narrow.

Graeme: I see 'em.

He turns the camera. Farmland bordered by a wall of trees on the other side of the windshield. Pockets of recovery sprinkled with reminders that the days of living death are far from over. Skeletal remains wrapped in tatters sprout from thriving grassland like calcified weeds. Buildings and vehicles abandoned and burnt out and vandalized.

A handful of undead amble eastward. One or two of them cast curious eyes toward the sound of the passing van's engine. The camera moves in, past the eastward march, toward the wall of trees, further back. An indelible shape haunts the open spaces between the rows; people, once living, now living-dead. They stand, half-hidden by wooden stanchions and the lower shrubs that congregate at the trees' bony, finger-knuckled roots.

Jules (V.O.): They stay mostly in the trees now, almost as if they've learned to fear open spaces where they could be easily picked off. You get enough of 'em together—like in the big cities—and it's a different story.

Jules: Musta been some activity come through here recently. Not sure if that's a good or a bad thing.

Hollister: Nobody's gonna fuck with us in this beast.

9

Jules (V.O.): Holly was right to call this thing a beast. What you have is essentially a Ford Sportsmobile 4-wheel-drive wrapped in Spectra Shield, Ballistic Nylon and bulletproof glass, and off-road front and rear bumpers with full grille guards. A rear-mounted 12-Volt winch with an 18,000 lb capacity. Full perimeter LED light bars. A PA system with a pair of roof-mounted megaphones. You name it. All sitting on top of Rugged Compound Runflat tires. Whatever the fuck that means. We clipped her from Alex Zamora, the East Coast Porn King, when we high-tailed it from his bunker in Princeton. He was the guy behind those, "Plump Asses Sitting on Opened Palms," videos that were the shit in the late '80s. Don't act like you've never heard of 'em.

The van was built on a lark to navigate a theoretical post-apocalyptic wasteland. Some car-mod show that never aired because Zamora's affiliation with pornography spooked the advertisers. The thing had been sitting in his garage, ever since, along with his collection of classic cars.

The car-mod show was produced by the same team behind *Gun Godz*. They did an episode where they built me a special replica guitar to memorialize my old axe GiGi. You remember GiGi? She was my first electric guitar. A candy apple red Les Paul Standard that I swore was alive. I liked to imagine that she was infused with the soul of some tortured musician who never realized her dream. Maybe she died of a freak accident while GiGi was being built.

I lost my GiGi when the Holt Sound Studios in Philly burned down in 1989. That shit hit me hard, man. She was my first love. The diehards will remember all the flap I got about the '68 Strat with the maple neck that I used from then on. The critics whined that it affected our signature sound. They blamed it for our "decline." In hindsight, maybe they were right. But it was the favorite guitar of one James Marshall Hendrix. So, at the time, my thinking was that any change had to be for the best.

Live and learn...

GiGi 2.0 is more of a novelty than a real axe. She'll get the job done, but her 'modifications' made it hard to get a quality sound out of her, and she was a bitch with security at airports. I used to keep her in a custom-built glass box on the wall of my home in Chestnut Hill with a sign that read: IN CASE OF EMERGENCY BREAK GLASS! Now she lives in that cello case back there. Why a cello case for a Replica Les Paul Standard, you ask? Just wait.

The back roads give way to turnpike townships. The battered old ghosts of chain restaurants and gas station mini marts. Tumbleweeds of man-made refuse. Twice dead bodies piled in parking lots.

The undead meander on the sidelines. A brave few wander in the open. They react to the approaching van. They turn, and sway, and oddly lurch toward the engine's smooth bellow. Some make moves toward the nearest shelter.

The boys talk over the images.

Graeme (re: piles of bodies): Probably not a good idea to be piling them up this soon.

Jules: People are in a hurry to wake up from this nightmare. I don't blame 'em.

Hollister: Long time before the disposal trucks make it out this far. They're just getting started in the big cities.

Jules: I don't know. It seems to be keeping the rest of 'em back. Maybe they're onto something.

Jules (V.O.): There were other signs that Project Reboot was taking hold out here in the sticks. Unlike the turnpike, which was still, essentially, a parking lot, the roads out here had been cleared in a few of the counties we passed through. Bright colored collages painted on abandoned cars and buildings dressed up the horizon. Even the water tower prophets were showing signs of hope. I get caught up in the vibe.

11

A year ago, I had all but accepted the fact that the world was ending and we had front row seats to it. And now, here we are on our way to the Weather to rock the fuck outta this deadfuck-infested planet. That's the Mount Weather Emergency Operations Facility in Bluemont, Virginia. Compliments of the President of the United States and the Martin Stone Radio Show. In case you live on Mars— which doesn't sound like such a bad idea at the moment— Martin Stone was a controversial Shock Jock who ruled the airwaves for as long as I can remember, and hands-down the best celebrity interviewer on the planet.

Holly turns up the volume on the stereo and starts rocking out to Sugerloaf's "Green-Eyed Lady." We used to cover the shit outta that tune in the old days. For the next 7:25 we rock out with him.

It's a nice little distraction from the elephant in the room, aka the Great Plains Settlement. Some idiot thought it would be a good idea to stop there on our way to the Weather. I'm looking at you, Holly.

More on that later…

Our lives have been a series of close calls since 9/6. We were commemorating our comeback album at Alex Zamora's place in Princeton when the shit hit the fan. It was going to coincide with the release of the film. We hadn't written a lick of music for the damn thing yet, but the fact that we had finally put aside all the bullshit for the sake of the group was a feat worth celebrating. Zamora was one of those guys whose obsession with doomsday preparation seemed a little nutty before 9/6. Nowadays you were lucky if you knew someone like that.

He had this badass bunker that no one knew about underneath his 4-acre estate. He called the place The Grotto. That's where we stayed until things got, well… complicated. Try to imagine being stuck in a single-story, 2800-square-foot space dressed up like an upscale condo along with the current queen of porn, who we nicknamed Cinderella, three washed-up, junkie actresses who were currently part of Zamora's harem of sister-wives. Then you had two animated mannequins who used to fuck these chicks on film. One of them couldn't get it up anymore and the other one's claim to fame was working as "stunt cock" for two A-list actors. Rounding out the group were four random associates of Zamora's who were each about as trustworthy as a record company exec on a good day. Top it off with one stoned-out-of-his-mind porn kingpin with a considerable arsenal at his disposal and a messiah complex that would've put Colonel Kurtz from *Apocalypse Now* to shame, and you've got a recipe for disaster.

Did I mention that one of the fucking associates was the porn queen's *Star 80* boyfriend?

It was doomed from the start. Me, Holly, and Gramps seemed to be the only ones aware of that fact. Zamora would stay in his bedroom surrounded by his sister-wives, who hated everything about Cinderella, especially all the attention she got from the other guys, including their husband. The mannequins and associates had each made a play at fucking her despite the best efforts of her *Star 80* boyfriend to derail that process. Of course, Cinderella only had eyes for Gramps. The sister-wives wanted a piece of him, too. But Gramps wanted no part of it. Between the three of us, we'd bagged enough top-shelf pussy during our run that a few months without it didn't seem to affect us the way it affected the others. Especially when the alternative is sticking your cock in the garbage, which is what screwing any of Zamora's girls amounted to.

It was too bad really. The place itself was fucking balls out! Zamora had spared no expense. Solar powered generator. A fully stocked walk-in freezer. Flatscreen monitors made to look like windows. They worked together to broadcast a continuous outdoor scene. Sounds silly, but it helped you forget that you were actually sealed up in a box seven-feet underground. There was an elaborate closed circuit TV system, which we later found out Zamora had been using to spy on everyone. A gym. A weapons room. Tons of camera equipment and a state-of-the-art editing suite/screening room where he shot, cut, and screened some of his more controversial films. The *Hatefuckers* series comes to mind.

Much of the film you're watching was shot using Zamora's equipment. That was Gramps doing his best Jim Forbes in the intro, by the way. Forbes was the voice behind *VH1's Behind the Music*. Always hated the one they did on us.

Zamora had this antique Celtic throne in his bedroom, just to give you an idea... He would go on and on about the damned thing.

"Just imagine the asses that've warmed that seat," he'd say. And I'm thinking, "*Not enough to make it worth the 200k you shelled out for it.*"

He had this ritual where he'd sit in the thing. An assortment of hardcore narcotics laid out buffet-style on this fancy-pants, stone coffee table. Then he'd go down the line, from right to left, until he was so fucking smashed that he would sometimes forget who you were.

Me and the guys had been clean for almost a year up to that point and we had no intention of falling back into the shitstorm of addiction, even if the idea of escaping reality was more appealing than ever. These days a clear head is essential to your survival.

The three of us had initially tossed around the idea of mutiny rather than leave our cushy accommodations. It was a few months in. The height of the collapse. It was starting to look like the deadfucks had won. Information from the outside world was minimal. The last we had heard from the Emergency Broadcast System was essentially, "You're on your own, folks."

"Green-Eyed Lady" skips and then cuts off. A skittering, whirling sound pours from the van's speakers. Hollister angrily jabs a button with his finger.

14

Hollister (re: CD player): No fucking way!

Hollister ejects the compact disk and looks it over. He blows on one side, rubs it against his shirt, and then slides it back into the console. He pushes a button and waits. The disc skitters and whirls. Silence...

Hollister ejects the CD and tosses it over his shoulder. It lands in a cardboard box on the floor near Jules' feet. The box is full of discarded CDs collected from various places along the way.

Hollister: So much for tunes, fellas.

Graeme: Shit, man!

Hollister: Oh. Wait...

Hollister reaches between the driver-seat and the center console and pulls out a CD. He blows on it and then holds it up for everyone to see.

Hollister (re: CD): G & R. "Appetite."

Graeme: Yes, please...

Jules (excited): I vote for the Stone Show.

Hollister is intrigued by Jules' suggestion. He looks over at Graeme.

Hollister (to Graeme): You cool with that? It *HAS* been awhile since tuned in.

Jules: Right? We can save G & R for after.

Graeme is mildly disappointed.

Graeme: Ohhh-kaay...

Hollister gently places the CD into a rectangular alcove

below the stereo, and then fingers a few buttons on the console.

A soothing female voice (Raven Tremble - African American, 41) fills the interior of the van. She is the former co-host and current host of the Martin Stone Radio Show.

Jules (V.O.): I fall under Raven's spell as soon as I hear her voice. It's a comforting feeling, like the warmth of a woman's naked body on a cold night. A live woman, that is. Gramps was right there with me.

The telethon was in full swing at the Weather. The goal was to find more virus-resistant donors to grow the government's vaccine supply. They were in the middle of a survivor story from some celebrity whose voice none of us recognized.

Later, Raven gets choked up when a random caller mentions Martin Stone. They cut to commercial. Same fucking ads as last week. The Consortium of Able-Bodied Volunteers. Hager Portable Shelters. We quote the ZOM-B-GONE ad verbatim. Even Holly—Mr. Too-mature-for-that-kinda-shit—gets in on the fun.

"...ZOM-B-GONE STICKY BOMB PERSONAL EXPLOSIVE DEVICE! ZOM-B-GONE STICKY BOMB PERSONAL EXPLOSIVE DEVICE! ZOM-B-GONE STICKY BOMB PERSONAL EXPLOSIVE DEVICE!"

We have a good laugh.

"We should cover that shit," Gramps jokes.

Raven apologizes when the show returns from break. She makes a few statements about the search for Martin Stone, which, as of this moment, has been unsuccessful. It's been 11-months since he called in to the show. Raven plays the infamous phone call for what must be the millionth time. We listen on pins and needles... again.

Heavy Static. Three words. "Raven. It's Martin." Dialtone.

Not everyone is convinced that the voice on the phone belonged to the real Martin Stone. But Raven had made up her mind. And that was all most people needed. Myself included.

She urges people to have hope and not to believe the rumors. There were three popular rumors going around.

Rumor #1: Martin Stone is dead, killed soon after the call.

As much as I love him, Martin would be the first to admit that he's a giant pussy who wouldn't last a minute in the trenches with the deadfucks. Maybe he's even walking round with the rest of 'em. There are people out looking for him, if you can believe that.

Rumor #2: Martin has been kidnapped and is currently being held hostage to use as a bargaining chip for the Lazarus vaccine.

LZ is more valuable than gold these days. The government caravans are constantly being raided. Virus resistant donors kidnapped on their way to the Weather. But if this one was true, I think we would have heard from the kidnappers by now.

Rumor #3: Martin is safe and sound at the Weather, where he's been since soon after the call. The government is manufacturing the 'missing' angle to rally support.

There was no denying Martin Stone's role in getting us through this thing. Who woulda thought? Radio Shock Jock Martin-fucking-Stone, savior of the human race. It was no accident that Raven and the survivors from the fall of the Brand Compound were allowed into the Weather and that the show was currently broadcast from there. The government meant to use that influence to reconnect with the nation. But as far as manufacturing the 'missing' angle... Not likely.

We didn't know about the Stone Show until the night of the big blowout at the Grotto between Cinderella and one of the sister-wives. I mean, we had developed a good rapport with Stone from the few times we did his show in the late

17

80s/early 90s, so we obviously knew who he was, but we had no idea that he was still broadcasting. Zamora had kept us in the dark. He wouldn't let anyone else into the communications room, so we got all our info second-hand. At the time, we had no reason not to trust him.

The fight between the girls was over whose room they were going meet in to listen to the Stone Show. I'm like, "Stone Show? As in Martin Stone?"

The girls agreed to let us listen under the condition that we not reveal to Zamora that they had been "borrowing" the satellite radio without his permission.

By the time we tuned in, the show had already become a movement. We learned about the other survivors out there. Heard their stories. I had no idea there were so many. People fighting back. Forming settlements. Trying to move forward with some sense of normalcy.

Things were going downhill fast at the Grotto, so we created the "gigs for food/supplies" ads that aired on the Stone Show. The idea was that we'd secretly try to work those gigs into an extended residency—hopefully permanently—at a decent settlement. We told Zamora that we just wanted to work out some new material. He was too obsessed with his filmography to listen to the Stone Show. He let us use his equipment under two conditions.

Condition #1: We had to let Cinderella contribute during the sessions.
That girl was to music what granny porn is to hard cocks—unless you're some kinda weirdo. Three failed albums—all produced by Zamora—and they still didn't get the hint.

Condition #2: We had to change our name to AntiRot.
Zamora thought it was so fucking clever. "You need a name people can get behind," he goes. We fought him on it, but it was obvious that short of killing him—which we considered—we would have to give in.

Before anything could pan out from the ads, things came to a head between Zamora and the *Star 80* boyfriend. Shots were fired. People took sides, which only made things worse. Dumb fucks never learn. There was only one side at the Grotto.

We came up with a plan. Gramps would take one for the team with one of the sister-wives. She was the worse one, too. This chick looked like she literally ate cigarettes. Gramps got her to slip Zamora a Mickey so they could be together. Then he was to get the codes to the freezer, garage, and the weapons room from her, and we'd be outta there lickety-split. Turned out Zamora was so paranoid that his wives didn't even know the code to the weapons room. So we had to settle for two-outta-three. We left that night while everyone slept. We left that shitty name behind, too.

The deadfucks were out in droves. It was a diverse crossroads of folks wandering around like awestruck tourists without an itinerary. Holly made a joke about racial harmony coming at a price, and another about the van's off-road grille guards being the great unifier or something. We moved through Jersey on slow steamroll, making forced conversation to distract from the constant bumpity-bump of soft bodies against the grille guards, the squishy crackling when the tires rolled them over, the pounding of hundreds of fists against the sides of the van, and the sound of as many voices grunting, and growling, and moaning, and wailing, and sounding all kinds of pissed that a hearty meal was very slowly getting away.

The windshield wipers couldn't move fast enough to clear away the blood before another coat darkened the glass. We could barely see through. We got our bearings with each sway of the wiper-arm, our faces pressed together like a *Three Stooges* bit, waiting for a peek through the temporary triangle of clarity, past the swell of deadfucks, at the road underneath their feet. The damn things were so tightly packed that it was hard to tell where the road ended and the dirt-shoulder began.

19

That was when we first saw our number one fan; a dead girl wrapped in soaking wet clothing—ripped jeans, boots, and a sleeveless concert t-shirt from our *"Ride the Serpentine"* Tour back in '87. Wet blond hair clinging to her porcelain-white face. She was hanging out with the stragglers a few layers into the woods up ahead where the road curved hard left. She appeared to be looking right at us, which, at the time, fit right in with the general deadfuck groupthink.

If it weren't for her groupie digs, and the concert Tee, we might've looked right past her. Just another deadfuck, albeit one who maintained a certain degree of beauty, even in death. A glimpse was all we could afford as there were far more pressing matters to attend to.

We were so slogged down with bodies... the under carriage, and wheel-well so mucked up with loose flesh, and shattered bone, and tangled in guts that, for a moment there, it seemed like we might not make it. And for the first time since this whole thing started, I worried that I might actually experience what it's like to be eaten alive. You can't imagine the rush of unholy terror that thought brings about. Not unless you've been there.

No sooner did things clear up than we stopped to help some "injured" couple on the side of the road and nearly got pinched by a group of scavengers.

Shoulda known... Shoulda-fucking-known...

Gramps was halfway outta the van when Holly stomped on the gas. The fuckers appeared from the trees seconds later. Like ninjas. Or is it ninja? It must've been a dozen of 'em, armed with automatic weapons. Gramps had to hang on for dear life as they fired at the van. Thank God for Spectra Shield, Ballistic Nylon, and bulletproof glass. We laugh about it now. At the time we seriously considered returning to the Grotto.

We ultimately decided to head to my place in Chestnut Hill, where I had a considerable gun collection stored in a safe behind a fake wall in my bedroom closet. It was nothing compared to Zamora's arsenal, but I've been shooting since I was a kid, so I had my share. That was why the *Gun Godz* crew modified GiGi 2.0 the way they did. She was there, too, by the way. Tucked away until I could get around to fixing her. Some problem with the firing mechanism.

The place was completely ransacked. It broke my heart to see it that way. This was my home. It looked like someone had gone through it with a sledgehammer and then celebrated with the party-to-end-all-parties. Graffiti everywhere. Broken glass. Holes kicked or punched in the walls throughout the house. A few bodies. Thank God they hadn't found the safe. We grabbed the guns, and a few other things, and booked.

Thanks to the Stone Show, we had the latest settlement list from the Emergency Broadcast System. So we headed toward the nearest settlement and crossed our fingers. We came across those scavengers again. Someone had left their heads on sticks on the side of Township Line Road. What goes around comes around, I guess.

The thing about celebrity is that people feel like they know you. And familiarity carries a lotta weight these days. It allowed us to sidestep that initial period of mistrust people talk about when you arrive at a new settlement. Sometimes they'd ask us to play, and we would gladly oblige with an acoustic set. Nine times outta ten they'd invite us to stay, and for a while things would go smoothly.

But then we'd eventually end up on the wrong end of a deadly weapon, usually in the hands of some rightly pissed-off boyfriend or husband out for blood because his lady fell under Gramps' spell. Most of the time the kid wasn't even trying. It's like a bonafide superpower, that fucking charm-a-his. Even at 48. And it ain't just the groupie-types that fall victim. I've seen it work on educated women. Doctors. Corporate CEOs. Assistant District Attorneys. The kinds-a-chicks you'd think would consider themselves above spreadin' for a rock star. Once he works that serpentine swagger, flips that hair-a-his, and flashes that crooked

21

smile, they all drop their drawers. It's the damndest thing. Even the dead ones...

Nah. I'm just fucking around. But damned if Gramps didn't occasionally spot some chick he'd bagged wandering around, post mortem. I shit you not. That boy got around.

If it wasn't Gramps' charm, then we'd wind up in the middle of some internal squabble that turned violent and/or led to some act of sabotage, and we'd have to book on a moment's notice. It never failed. Ever.

Altogether, we had been asked to leave, thrown out of, or escaped from seven settlements. It became obvious to us that we needed our own place.

We had our instruments, a few guns, a 5lb bag of Idaho Russets, and a case of outdated Spaghettios to our name. The food was compliments of our last place of residency. A real shithole group in Somerset, Pa.

"Looks like liquid shits on the horizon for us," I joked.

Holly gets all pissy, goes, "At least we have food."

Good ole Professor Buzzkill. Holly's the straight-man of our crew, in case you couldn't tell by now. The Costello to me and Gramps' Abbott. The Martin to our Lewis. The Murtaugh to our Riggs.

We took a vote and decided that our best option was to head back to the Grotto. It was two-to-one; Holly being the odd man out.

It had been roughly six months since we left the place. In that time, there was no way, in hell, that band of fucktards hadn't killed each other or, in some way, gotten themselves killed. No fucking way. It was a statistical impossibility.

Holly was butthurt about finding our friends—and I use the term lightly—walking around all deadfucked.

22

I kept busting his balls on the ride there. "No gig is too small," I go. It used to be our motto when we were starting out. Now it stands for any fucked up, shitball situation where we're faced with less than favorable odds.

Holly had a point, actually. It's always worse when it's someone you know behind that deadfuck gaze. Especially when you have to waste 'em. It messes with your head in a way that you never get used to. I don't give a fuck how desensitized you think you are. You start to second guess yourself as you lock them in your sights. It may have only been hours ago that you were having a conversation with this person. And now they want to eat you. And not in the good way.

You wonder. "Was that just recognition I saw in their eyes? Is there some hint of the person I knew just hours, minutes, seconds ago, begging me not to shoot?"

Everyone hears that voice. But again, I would hardly call anyone at the Grotto a friend. Maybe Zamora, in the beginning. Maybe... But even he had an agenda, which was...

1: To promote his girls. We stocked all our early videos with the bimbos.

2: To jam with us. Zamora had rock-star aspirations without a lick of talent in that regard.

"And what if they *did* survive?" Holly goes on to say. "You think Zamora's just gonna welcome us back? You think he's gonna let it slide that we stole his van or that we took food from the freezer? And let's say he's in a forgiving mood... Would you honestly want to live with those psychotic junkies again? What's your solution then? Huh? We just gonna ask them to leave? Er kick 'em out? Er kill them if they don't? You prepared for all that?"

Holly has a knack for the dramatics, if you haven't noticed.

We held out hope that whatever had gone down at the Grotto after we left, that they hadn't completely destroyed the place. Between the three of us, we're handy enough that we could make it livable as long as the damage wasn't too severe. Especially Holly. Give that boy a tool-belt and some time and he can fix just about anything. My father was like that, too.

The generator was still running when we got there. Zamora kept it hidden under a row of fake shrubs on the northeast side of the estate. Solar panels posed as skylights above the kitchenette. The front door to the main house had been left wide open. No sign of forced entry. Not good. Inside a few deadfucks wandering like prospective buyers at an open house. No sweat.

The entrance to the Grotto was locked from the inside, which meant they were still down there. The door was located underneath the fireplace. We knocked, but got no answer.

There was a back entrance upstairs in the master bedroom; a fake wall inside the armoire. It opened onto a stairwell that led to Zamora's room in the bunker. He let mention of it slip one night when the alcohol/OxyContin cocktail had him tripping balls.

Actually, that was every night.

It was a long trip down that staircase. We wet some towels and held them over our faces to block out the smell. It was so fucking bad it stung your eyes. If you think you're immune to deadfuck b.o., try to imagine it after being sealed in an enclosed area for six months. It gets in your clothes. Your hair. Up your nose. And it haunts you for days. Just the thought of it makes me wanna heave.

I found myself reexamining my feelings toward the Grotto group on the way down. If we weren't friends then why was my stomach all knotted up at the thought of seeing them deadfucked?

"Having second thoughts?" Holly goes. I must've had a look on my face.

The smell was even worse in Zamora's room. Thicker. Like it had weight to it, if that makes any sense. "Fruiting shit wrapped in rotten cold cuts," was Gramps' take on it. And he wasn't far off. It was the kinda thing you had to prepare yourself for. You couldn't just run in. Even with a towel over your face.

It took a second to register that the thing squeezed into Zamora's throne was even human, let alone the man himself. The Goddamned thing had to be three, maybe four times his size, and swollen from a mixture of food and death-bloat. His face was like an unflattering caricature, made into a mask, and then placed on top of a much bigger face. There was a column of rolls as wide as his fattened head where his neck used to be. Loose fat pushed through open spaces in the chair and spilled over the arms like rising dough.

The throne was surrounded by an altar of garbage. Empty cans. Plastic wrappers. Water bottles. Half-eaten meals on plates. Several of the plates were broken from the slide down the garbage slope.

We approached him from behind. Holly goes, "That you, Alex?"

Sounds funny in retrospect.

Zamora's reaction was delayed. Like he had overheard one stranger calling out to another across a crowded room and was mildly curious to put faces to the voices. His eyes eventually found us. They were clouded over and bugged out of his head in way that seemed to suggest life. For a split second I wondered. *"Is he...?"*

Then Gramps gets all Captain Obvious and lays it out CSI-style. "Looks like the weight gain put so much stress on his heart that he couldn't handle his usual drug cocktail," he goes.

Zamora's eyes light up. "Food!" I didn't think they could get any bigger.

If wood could scream it would sound something like the noise the throne made when he leaned toward Gramps, who was closest to him, and tried to grab him with his big sausage arms and hands that literally looked like over-inflated surgical gloves.

Holly walks up and plants a screwdriver right in his skull. Bye bye deadfuck-Zamora. We shared a quiet moment as you often do when it's someone you know... er knew. Something I forgot to mention earlier.

A fire lights under Holly's ass. He looks up, goes, "The others!" And we all have the same thought.

"Did the fat fucker eat them?"

"Nah..." I think I actually said it out loud.

Me and Holly head for the door to search for the others when Gramps yells, "Wait!"

He's got the TV remote in his hand. He points it at the screen and pushes "Play."

There they were; what was left of the group, duct-taped to chairs in the screening room. Cinderella. A sister-wife. The stunt cock and an associate. They were seated side-by-side. Clearly deadfucked. A movie played, on a loop, on the screen. Scenes from Zamora's latest, and probably his worst.

"Sick son of a bitch," Holly goes.

Zamora would have these movie nights. It started off as a good thing. We'd watch mostly upbeat flicks to escape from reality. Zamora would slip in some unused stuff from his archives and then pester you for your opinion afterward. The smart move was to lie. As time went on movie night turned into the Alex Zamora Film Festival. Attendance mandatory.

Graeme rewinds the footage.

"I'm not sure I wanna see this," Holly goes, but he doesn't look away when Gramps pushes "Play," again.

Video (Grotto CCTV Cam - Various - No Sound)

The Screening Room

A small screening room. Movie-theater-style seating. A screen spans the entire length and width of the front wall.

An obese, pajama-clad Zamora leads Cinderella, a sister-wife, the stunt-cock, and an associate into the room at gunpoint and instructs them to sit next to each other. They look weak, malnourished. The men appear to have been beaten. Their heads hang low. Shoulders slack. No fight left in them. The stunt-cock appears to have received the worst of it. He can barely stand and has to be helped into his seat.

Zamora puts the gun to Cinderella's head. She shrinks, face tightened, eyes squeezed shut. Tears stream down her face as she anticipates her demise. "Will it hurt? Will it be quick?"

Zamora savors the moment, and then yells something to the group. They flinch at the sound of his raised voice. He continues to yell and gesture toward the screen. Afterward, he leans closer to Cinderella and mouths something in her ear. He points at a plastic bag on the floor. Several rolls of duct tape inside. The girl grabs a roll and moves reluctantly to tape the others to their chairs. Zamora scrutinizes her technique along the way and threatens her several times for moving too slowly. She is trembling, weeping heavily. Afterward, he tapes the girl to the aisle seat using the same technique. He makes a point to do it twice as quickly as she had done. He makes a speech punctuated with big, sweeping arm movements, and then leaves the room.

Cinderella and the sister-wife struggle against their restraints and attempt to rally the others, but the stunt-cock is barely conscious and the associate is paralyzed by fear. He sits there, staring straight ahead and babbling something to himself. The sister-wife eventually yells at him to, "SHUT THE FUCK UP!"

The group looks toward the ceiling, reacting to the dimming lights. Nightvision kicks in and colors the view a putrid green. The movie-screen comes alive and startles the group. The Zamora Films logo fades to a shot of Zamora seated in a directors' chair dressed like some relic from Hollywood's Golden Age. He makes a high-minded speech and then unleashes a haphazard montage of extreme sexual acts on the audience.

Cinderella and the sister-wife curse at the screen and continue to struggle. Some of their own scenes appear in the montage. The associate has awakened from his fear-coma and is talking to the stunt-cock, who doesn't respond, but just sits there, motionless. Head sagging. Hang-jawed. Drool.

Cinderella and the sister-wife join in. Before long they are yelling at the barely conscious stunt cock to "HOLD ON! WAKE UP! STAY ALIVE!" No response. No movement. The associate leans in trying to get a look at the young man's face. The stunt-cock flinches, startling the associate. His head bounces. He looks up slowly, dead, but alive.

Undead stunt-cock drunkenly pivots his head from side-to-side as if to ascertain his surroundings. His eyes widen at the sight of food. He lunges toward the associate, and then the sister-wife, teeth snapping shut inches away from them. They panic, screaming, and fighting the restraints with more vigor. The undead stunt-cock thrashes against his restraints as if angered by them. He lunges at the sister-wife without warning. She leans away, but not fast enough, and he bites her on the shoulder. She cries out in pain as Undead stunt-cock snatches his head away from her, his mouth attached by elastic strands of flesh. Blood everywhere.

Fast Forward...

...the sister-wife's body is slouched in her seat, her head slumped toward the stunt-cock, who devours the left side of her face, biting, and whipping his head, and snatching chunks of meat away from the chewed visage. Cinderella weeps in her seat. The associate thrashes against his restraints.

Fast Forward...

...A frantic Cinderella leans away from Undead sister-wife's half-headed snarl and her snapping teeth. Her face twisted in palpable terror. The stunt-cock similarly pursues the associate.

Fast Forward...

An audience of four, seated side-by-side, seemingly content with each other and with the rapid-fire montage of depravity on the screen. They stare with slack-jawed wonder, mesmerized by the color-storm and the noise or maybe by the sight of warm, edible meat blown up to giant proportions. Cinderella and the associate are no longer interested in fighting. Their wounds tell the story of their demise— Cinderella with her left ear missing and her left arm dangling by sinewy strands from her shoulder. The associate with his entire face eaten away.

Video (Canon Vixia HF HD Camera)

Interior of van / scenery outside windows

Jules seated in back thumbing through a magazine. Acoustic guitar in his lap. Hollister and Graeme in the driver and passenger-seats respectively. Graeme has the window down. His arm rests on the frame.

Jules (V.O.): We got the codes to the entire place by watching footage of Zamora skulking around while everyone slept. Gramps' idea. We spent a whole day disposing of

29

Zamora's body, which we had to freeze, and then cut into pieces. Another day on the rest of the group. We drew straws to see who would have to... de-deadfuckify them, shall we say, and who would have to cut up Zamora. The honors went to Gramps and Holly, respectively. In the end, we did it together. No way I was gonna let them have all the fun. Goooo teamwork!

We piled the bodies out back and burned them. The fire pushed the deadfucks back to the wall of trees that bordered Zamora's estate. We fired off a few rounds in the air to remind the hard-headed ones who's boss. If they had half-a-brain they'd realize that they had us outnumbered. The fuckers had been creeping since we returned, circling the fringes of the estate like sharks on ketamine. "Looks like we're gonna have to do some cleaning," I go.

"I could use the target practice," Holly says.

We all could.

We said a little prayer for the group as the fire raged on. None of us are even remotely religious, but it felt like the right thing to do. We're doin' the whole "moment-of-silence" thing, when Gramps goes, "Please tell me you can see that?"

Me and Holly look up, unsure which one of us he's talking to. He's looking toward the trees. So, we look, too.

"Over there," he goes. "The tree lying on its side..."

But I had already spotted her; our number one fan. The area had been hit with a monster storm a few days before we arrived. An old tree trunk, hollowed out from rot, lie on its side, victim of the wind. The dead girl was standing on top of it like some kinda lookout for the deadfuck army meandering in the woods around her. And as usual, she was looking in our direction. They all were, in fact. But there was a difference in the way she stared. The others seemed more interested in the flames than the scruffy-looking Rock 'n'

30

Roll Dinosaurs standing in front of it. But not her.

You could literally feel her eyes on you. It still gives me the chills. Don't know if you've ever had the privilege of sharing your living space with cockroaches, and I'm talking the big German kind. Just the sight of one haunts you for hours. Especially if it gets away. You know it's there, but you can't see it. Meanwhile it sits there, waiting for an opportunity to crawl up your pant-leg or across your plate or onto the bed while you're sleeping. That kind thing.

"So I *wasn't* seeing things." Holly goes as if a weight had suddenly lifted off his shoulders. I was thinking the same thing, to be honest.

It took us three more days to get the Grotto back to livable condition. Zamora had put a pretty good dent in the food, but there was a few months' worth of canned vegetables, Ramen noodles, and oatmeal to go with our supply of potatoes and Spaghettios. Yum!
After several attempts to get rid of the smell, we gave up on Zamora's room, and sealed it off from the rest of the bunker.

During that time we shared stories about our number one fan. Each of us had seen her since that day 6-months-ago when we bolted from the Grotto. Come to find out, Gramps had even attempted to communicate with the girl at one point.

"It was back at Somerset," he goes. "Behind the old church, just outside the perimeter of the compound. The one by the lake."

"Tha Hell were you doing way out there?" I say.

"The black chick," Holly goes as if I should've known.

He's right. I should've known. Her and Gramps' quickie behind the church was the reason we were "asked" to leave the place. Turned out the girl was spoken for. By whom, was the question? There were two people laying stake to that claim. Three if you count the leader's wife. I often wonder how that ended. Probably not good.

"Her name was Siobhan," Gramps says like he had real feelings for her or something. "After we screwed, I bummed a cigarette from her and stayed out there and smoked it after she went back inside," he goes. "That's when I saw the girl. She was standing at the edge of the lake, looking up the hill at me. This was maybe the third time I had seen her since we left the Grotto. I thought it was all in my head. You know? I was afraid to say anything and have you guys start looking at me sideways."

We had each arrived at a similar conclusion from our individual encounters with the dead girl in the soaking wet groupie digs and the "*Ride the Serpentine*" Concert Tee. No use mentioning it to the others and raising concern about your mental state and/or risk losing the trust of the only people in the world that you trust. These days trust is about as rare as chicks with shaved cooches.

"It was a real secluded spot me and Siobhan had picked," Gramps goes. "No other deadfucks in sight. So, I'm like, 'I need to deal with this.' For the sake of my sanity, at least. Right? So, I walk closer to the chick. She doesn't move. I ask her; 'Can you hear me? Who are you? What do you want from us?' She looks at me like she wants to tell me something…"

"Yeah. Come over here pretty-boy and let me eat your skinny ass," I say to lighten the mood.

But Gramps was lost in the memory. He talks right over me.

"I walk closer," he continues. "I get within 10-feet of the chick and she starts walking toward *me*. The look on her face changes. Almost like she's happy. But happy like a cult-member about to drink the Kool Aid. She's like… smiling through a peaceful expression. I can see that her eye-makeup is smeared from crying. When's the last time you saw a deadfuck cry? Right? She opens her mouth like she's about to say something, but it just kinda hangs open."

Then the son of a bitch trails off with me and Holly sittin' firmly on the edges of our seats.

"Then what?" We say it almost simultaneously.

"Then I ran is what I fucking did!"

"Weren't you packin?" I go.

"I had the Glock."

"Why didn't you just plug her then?"

"I don't know. Something about her. I can't put my finger on it. I just felt like I needed to get away from her."

Remember what I said about cockroaches? Imagine being bitch-slapped by the physical manifestation of that vibe.

I couldn't sleep that night. I must've lay there for hours with the lights on, scrolling through the same three questions over and over in my head.

1: Who the hell is this girl?

2: How the fuck does she keep finding us?

3: How is it that she always looks the same?

Six months is a lifetime in deadfuck years. If they even survived that long, you'd expect a certain degree of rot or some gaping, oozing memento of his or her death or of some encounter with the living.

Lights-out in the Grotto was a special kind of dark. Sensory deprivation dark. You want to wait until you're dead-tired before turning in. No pun intended. If you weren't asleep within the first few minutes then you were liable to be taken to places you'd rather not explore. Absolute darkness and absolute silence provides the perfect platform for a fractured psyche to run free. I made the mistake of turning in on half-a-tank. But I was determined to will myself to sleep and *NOT* to dream. Short of death, it's the only escape from this Hell.

I was on the waking end of a nod-off cycle when I heard a noise like a faint tapping in the distance. I thought… I hoped it was one of the boys up for a late-night piss, but there were no residual sounds to support that scenario.

I hear the sound again. I lay there and listen. Was it coming from the main entrance of the Grotto? Maybe someone knocking on the main door? My heart sank. That "someone" would have to know exactly where to look to find the entrance. Then they'd have to remove the fake fireplace display and lift the panel of steel flooring underneath it to reach the door, which resembles the hatch on a submarine.

A seemingly headless Holly appears at my doorway and scares the shit outta me. But he's only wriggling into his shirt. "Someone's at the main entrance," he says, pushing his head through the neck-hole.

My brain spits out a stupid question, "Who?"

"How, the fuck, should I know. A friend of Zamora's?"

"That's just what we fucking need."

"Come on."

He calls out to Gramps as he heads off toward the control room. I jump out of bed and into my clothes. Something on the monitors has Holly and Gramps' undivided attention when I reach the control room. I shove my way between them and have a look.

It's her. Our number one fan. She's down on one knee by the fireplace. A puddle of water on the floor underneath her. The fake display is spread across the living room. The steel flooring lifted onto one side exposing the main entrance door. She knocks again.

Tap! Tap! Tap!

And then she waits. We stand there in silence trying to process what we were seeing.

"I vote we put her creepy ass down before she attracts more of 'em," I go. We had yet to clean up the area and it was getting thick with deadfucks. That's when they're the most dangerous.

"How do we know this isn't some trick just to get us to come outside?" Holly says.

"A trick?" I go. "Are you fucking kidding me? Orchestrated by who? Rod-fucking-Serling?"

The girl knocks and waits again. Meanwhile me and Holly bicker like a married couple. Afterward she stands up, turns, and looks directly at the camera.

It was like somebody let all the air out of the room. The camera in the living room, which is about the size of an AA battery, is hidden in a vent. There was no way she could've known that.

She stands there for a good minute, and then she turns and walks out through the sliding doors on the east side of the house all Michael Myers-like. Holly turns on the exterior floodlights and switches to the cameras mounted high up on the light posts. We watch the girl wander out into the east yard.

Now the argument between me and Holly becomes about whether or not we should go after her and put a period on this whole thing. We hadn't even noticed that Gramps had left the room until...

Movement on one of the monitors...

It pulls my attention away from the intellectual bullshit falling out of Holly's mouth. I look and see Gramps taking long strides across the east lawn like a hound-dog locked on a scent. He's plugging deadfucks like it's an afterthought, letting them get dangerously close before pulling the trigger, and doing so without even looking. He's armed with a Glock 19. That's 15 rounds versus three times as many deadfucks. At least.

Holly throws attitude my way on his way out the room, "Happy now?"

Video (Grotto CCTV Cam – Various)

East Yard

An overhead view of a 1-acre field boxed in by Spartan Juniper trees and gaudy, Romanesque sculptures atop faux Corinthian columns. The tatters of a volleyball net hangs sadly between rusted steel posts. A gazebo meant to resemble ancient ruins. Floodlights on tall posts impaled in the dirt. Three on each side of the yard, spaced 10-feet apart. A camera mounted on each one.

Upright corpses materialize from the spaces between junipers. More pour in from around the front of the estate. They converge in the middle, a sedated stampede, hive-minded, hungry-eyed, and salivating at the source of their heightened aggression.

Graeme Gunz moves with purpose toward a gap in the juniper wall. A trailed of bodies laid out in his wake. An unruly crowd hot on his trail. An ambitious young corpse lunges from the side. Graeme caps it without missing a step. His focus, on the stone pathway winding off into the woods, locked in and unwavering. A headless bust stationed on either side of the pathway. Darkness beyond the trees…

Jules and Hollister explode from the East doors armed with M16s. A canvas satchel strapped across Jules' torso. They run out into the yard and immediately take aim…

36

Hollister: GREAME!

Jules (to Graeme): What the hell're you doing, Man?!

They work to thin the herd of undead, starting with the ones closest to Graeme. They move toward Graeme's position, firing away. A misty cloud-canopy of exploded cerebral residue rains down, painting heads and shoulders red. The herd marches forward like some tribe of stiff-jointed, lead-limbed berserkers worked into a frenzy and covered in war paint. They are unfazed by the bodies dropping all around them and by the obstacles those bodies present. The idea of warm flesh is just too intoxicating. A small faction of undead changes direction, like a deformed tentacle extending away from a larger body and reaching for the two armed men standing on the sideline of the stampede.

Graeme is standing at the mouth of the stone pathway now. His arms hanging by his sides. Shoulders slack. His right hand wrapped around the handle of his gun. Just beyond the junipers, a shadowy figure moves toward the light. Seconds later, a dead man in blood-stained medical scrubs and a face-mask of third-degree burns steps through the gap. His pace quickens, he reaches out to Graeme, fingers flexing and curling into claws.

Graeme stands there, posture on Mesmer. His body language suggests that he has every intention of allowing the undead man in scrubs to approach him.

Hollister turns his weapon on the approaching undead. He takes out a few before his gun clicks empty.

Hollister (to Jules): I'm out!

Jules reaches into his satchel and tosses a clip to Hollister. He grabs another clip from the satchel. As he reloads his gun...

Jules: GRAAAAAEEEEME!!! (to Hollister) What's he doin'?!

Hollister shakes his head, "I dunno…"

Graeme doesn't respond. Instead, he opens his arms to the undead man in scrubs and third degree burns. The man staggers closer, all gums and gnashed teeth shining through an oblong ball of charred meat that used to be a face.

Scrubs is just about on Graeme when Jules takes a shot and then, in one motion, he returns to clearing the herd. Scrubs' head jerks violently to the right. Blood. Graeme whips his face away from the harsh, wet kiss of airborne brain matter. Scrubs crumbles to the ground, leaking moist chunks from the jagged hole in the top, left side of his head.

Graeme (re Scrubs): Noooooo!

Graeme turns and charges at Jules, a madman covered in undead blood. Jules catches wind at the last minute…

Jules (re: Graeme): Hey! What the fu—

…and moves to defend himself against the lanky, pretty-boy juggernaut. The two men tussle.

Graeme: Why'd you have to kill her?

Hollister hurries over and divides his time between separating Jules and Graeme and keeping the herd momentarily at bay. He manages to get between them, wraps his arms around a thrashing Graeme and walks him backward, away from Jules.

As Graeme continues to thrash…

Graeme: Why'd you fucking kill her?! She was trying to communicate with me you stupid fuck!

Jules nonchalantly picks of a few undead between gestures of disbelief.

Jules: Well, excuse me for saving your skinny ass!

Graeme: I had it under control! She wasn't going to hurt me!

Hollister fires a few rounds with equal disregard and then leans into Graeme's line of sight.

Hollister: Whaddayou mean, she? She, who?

Graeme points to Scrubs' expired corpse lying prone in the dirt.

Graeme: The girl... Our fan...

Jules fires without looking. A few undead drop.

Jules (to Graeme): Tha fuck are you talking about?

Graeme eyes Jules with suspicion.

Graeme: Waaait a minute, now. I thought we all agreed she was real.

Hollister calmly drops a few more undead and then grabs Graeme by the shoulders and points him in the direction of Scrubs' body.

Hollister: We did. But that ain't her.

Video (Canon Vixia HF HD Camera)

Interior of van / scenery outside windows

Jules seated in back. Hollister and Graeme in the driver and passenger-seats respectively.

Jules (V.O.): There were so many deadfucks. The damn things were coming out of the woodwork faster than we could plug 'em. We couldn't chance having them follow us inside, so we led them away from the estate and ducked into a house down the road where we settled for the night and waited for them to lose interest. Turned out the place used to belong to that basketball player who was outed as a furry by one of the gossip rags. Damn near killed his career. Wouldn't you know, he had a photo of himself with Zamora in his den. Figures.

The place had been thoroughly ransacked and looted to shit, but the doors and windows were mostly intact. We found a stash of liquor hidden in a heap of boxes in the basement. Medicine for the night. Gramps snagged the Patron. Holly took the Jack Daniels and I was packin' a fancy-schmacy bottle of Absolute Citron.

"I know what you're both thinking," Gramps goes once the Tequila kicks in. "But I'm not slipping. I'm fine."

"Nobody thinks you're slipping," Holly says.

"I would if I was in you guys' shoes."

"We all saw the girl on the monitor," I go.

"I'm not talking about the monitor. She was there in the east yard, too. Standing right in front of me. Not more than 10-feet away. I threatened to put a bullet between her eyes unless she came clean. She just gives me this look, same as before. Then she takes off her clothes and starts walking toward me. I knew what was happening was fucked, but it was like I couldn't move. When you plugged her... It felt like... like being jarred awake from a deep sleep."

We must've sat there for an hour, taking long swigs and not knowing what to say. With everything we knew about this girl, we had no reason not to believe Gramps' story. But what did it mean? Holly was the first one to offer up a theory.

"What if she's a ghost?" he says like he expected us to laugh in his face. No one did.

Gramps nods like he's on the same page and has been for some time.

"Why not a ghost. Right?" Holly continues, enlivened by

Gramps' nodding endorsement and half a bottle of Jack. "We live in a world where dead people come back to life and eat living people. How fucked is that? So, why, the fuck, not? Why not Chupacabres, too? And fairies. And Leprechauns. And fucking... Bigfoot sitting on a goddamn unicorn, surfing a UFO across the Bermuda-fucking-triangle?"

I raise my bottle in support. "Why, the fuck, not!" I take a drink then add, "Maybe not Leprechauns, though."

"What does she want?" Gramps steps all over my comic-timing like not knowing causes him great pain.

"I think it's obvious what would've happened if Jules hadn't taken the shot," Holly says.

"But why?"

"That's the million dollar question, kid."

Holly goes on to theorize that we only seem to see her in the presence of deadfucks, like she somehow uses them to travel around. Sounds kinda cool if it wasn't so Goddamn unsettling.

I take a long swig and grunt away the burning aftertaste. Afterward, I whip my head toward an imaginary camera somewhere between Holly and Gramps and go into my best Clint Eastwood. "Looks like we got some cleaning up to do," I say.

Nobody laughs.

Tough crowd.

Video (Grotto CCTV Cam – Various)

Weapons room

Antiseptic lighting. Several long weapons (assault rifles, shotguns, rpgs) mounted vertically on the wall. Another wall for handguns. Another for miscellaneous gear (holsters, slings, vests, shell-bags). A cabinet full of ammo.

Quick cuts of Graeme and Hollister reaching into the frame and snatching weapons from the walls.

Garage roof

A six car-garage the size of a modest house. A wide driveway down in front extends to the edge of the frame and beyond. An overgrown field borders the other sides of the garage. A wooden deck on top. Expensive patio furniture shoved aside. Jules standing in the middle of the deck, dowsed in sunlight. A guitar strapped to his chest. A wire snakes from the butt of the guitar to a mid-sized amplifier on the deck. A large speaker in the corner. Chirping chords waft from the guitar as Jules tunes the strings. A loose contingent of undead stumble into the frame from all sides and make their way toward the noise, the slow-lurch parade seemingly in accord with the fragmented rhythm.

Jules (V.O.): I hurt my knee in the tussle with Gramps, so the boys thought I should hang back while they cleaned up. Holly came up with what you see here when I pitched a fit about Plan A. The speaker and amp were compliments of Zamora's rock star pipe dream. The idea was that I act as a decoy to lure the deadfucks out into the open and help round 'em up into one location. Then Gramps and Holly would come in and cut 'em down. It gave me the opportunity to shred, which I had been complaining about not having had in a while. Wished it was with GiGi, but she was still laid up with a jammed firing mechanism. I felt guilty for neglecting her.

Weapons room

Graeme and Hollister clad in tactical gear. They strap weapons across their torsos and slide handguns into their holsters.

Garage roof

The chirping chords become more succinct as Jules finds his perfect pitch. His fingers dance, translating kinetic energy into sound. Slow, seductive chords like foreplay for some monumental sexual event. Jules sinks in the groove. The chords manifest in swaying movement and a rhythmic head-nod, scraggy red hair hanging in front of his face. A crowd forms at the foot of the raised stage, growing exponentially through a series of scene dissolves...

Soon the garage is surrounded by a pulsating, undulating skirt of undead, their intent splayed across their rotten faces as they reach upward and claw and bite at air, laying hands on the garage walls as if to find purchase and climb up.

Jules is locked in a symbiotic link with his guitar, seemingly unconcerned with the crowd beneath him. His eyes squeezed shut. Head nodding. Hips grinding air. Fingers doing a dexterous dance on the strings while the bridge squeals to his slow-hand caress.

Gunshots ring out off-camera. A shift in the undead crowd as bodies begin to drop. The phenomena spreads out from the rear of the garage, around to the sides...

Graeme and Hollister enter the frame from rear-left and right. They are nearly unrecognizable wrapped in battle gear and brandishing machine guns—an AR 15 and an MK 17, respectively. Several more guns on their person. A designer golf-club (a driver) dangles upside-down from Graeme's belt. The wrapped handle of an aluminum tee-ball bat protrudes from a long carrying case strapped to Hollister's back. Bandanas around their necks. Goggles.

The two men press forward, their torsos on pivot like an automatic sprinkler, spraying the crowd with bullets. It becomes evident that they are targeting the lower extremities. A follow up headshot as the bodies drop—if possible. Graeme moves left, Hollister right. They travel at an arc, around the sides, to the front of the garage, and come together in the middle of the driveway.

43

Jules continues to play as the bodies fall and lay splayed out, writhing like dying petals on some giant, fleshy flower. Down below, Graeme and Hollister have stopped firing to inspect the damage. A few dozen undead remain among the moist, slushy carrion moat at the base of the garage, unable to stand, yet still determined to nab the nearest bite of warm flesh.

Graeme and Hollister strap their primary weapons across their torsos. Graeme yanks the driver from his waist and flips it right-side up. Hollister slides the bat from the carrying case against his back. They pull the bandanas over their mouths and noses and communicate via nods before wading into the moat. They swing their weapons like bludgeons at the heads of any surviving undead, high-stepping so as not to slip on the soft, squishy chunks that moved strangely underfoot or to become entangled in the intestinal lattice.

Video (Canon Vixia HF HD Camera)

Interior of van / scenery outside windows

Jules seated in back. Hollister and Graeme in the driver and passenger-seats.

Jules (V.O.): Gramps and Holly both reported seeing our fan during the bitch of a clean-up. Some random deadfuck Holly was dragging to the burn-pile. One of the few that had managed to survive the bullet-spray and the blunt-object-beatdown.

"This one was like paralyzed from the neck down," Holly goes. "Just some average-looking fuck dressed like he was dead long before he was walking around jonesing for live meat. I was holding him by the legs. His arms were up over his head, which was turned to the side facing Gramps, who was dragging a body next to me."

Then Gramps chimes in.

"I look over and there she was staring at me while Holly

dragged her," he goes.

"Same shirt. Same ripped jeans. Same boots. All soaking wet. Hair clinging to her face. The whole shebang," Holly continues. "It was seriously fucked. I dropped the bitch like a hot potato. Had to ask myself if I had somehow mistaken the average fuck for this chick back at the garage, but I knew there was no way. Meanwhile Gramps goes apeshit and starts stomping the chick's face and head until there's nothing left. I had to pull him offa her. When we looked again it was the average fuck laying there with his face bashed in. Seriously fucked, man."

That was the last we saw of our fan for a long time. We settled on a plan-of-action should we see her again, which were essentially the same rules for dealing with deadfucks.

1: Keep your distance.

2: Aim for the head.

3: Avoid eye-contact

Within a week, she had fallen to the bottom of the list of daily concerns. Within two weeks, she was a haunted memory.

Video (Grotto CCTV Cam – Various / Canon Vixia HF HD Camera)

Grotto Montage

A montage of daily life at the Grotto.

We had settled into a routine. Morning stretch/workout. Breakfast with the Stone Show. Jam sessions. Movie night. Long discussions about the meaning of life and lack thereof—we each did time as Debbie Downer and Captain Optimism. We had become the poster children for the Post-9/6 American Family: Rockstar Edition.

I finally got around to fixing GiGi and was dying to play

with her. Gramps got on this filmmaking kick and starting recording everything. That was the official beginning of the documentary you're watching. He would spend hours in the editing suite learning how to use the equipment. The rest of the time he'd walk around with that damn Vixia stuck to his eye or playing around with Zamora's collection of spy cameras. There were cameras built into a pair of glasses, a baseball cap, pens, cell phones. It was like a creepy voyeur's paradise; all the shit Zamora had. Gramps has an addictive personality. So when he's into something— or someone—he's all in. His face lights up in a way that makes his enthusiasm infectious. Like when he would really connect with lyrics I wrote. So you're instantly drawn into whatever he's into at the moment.

Holly got in touch with his inner-Yoda through a series of books and videos we scavenged from one of the neighboring estates. Some Hedge Fund Guru's place. When he wasn't doing that, Holly spent whole days tinkering with things with that tool-belt-a-his. His latest project was rigging the Sportsmobile's PA system into an amp. "So we can roll into the Weather, guns blazing!" he said. "Guns" being a metaphor for "music," in this scenario, for all you people who need it spelled out.

Within a month we had an album's worth of new music. I'm talkin' the best shit we'd ever done. We didn't even realize what we had until we watched the footage from the jam sessions. Rock 'n' Roll was our therapy. It allowed us to work through all the bullshit.
The new stuff was a culmination of everything we had gone through since the world turned upside-down, put to music. We avoided using our number one fan as inspiration, out of fear that we might somehow conjure her up. I wrote a little something for her in secret, though. Just a few lines. My intention was to explore the person she was in life, but I was working with very little info.

We were listening to the Stone Show the morning the Brand Compound came under attack. We grieved when the show went dark. I would equate the feeling with withdrawal. We tuned in to the wannabees and the whack jobs to ease the pain. Word spread quickly about Mother Margaret and the Left Hand Cult and how they were behind the attack. They saw 9/6 as the literal interpretation of the biblical *Book of Revelations* and they were against any efforts to resist what *God* had set in motion. The general consensus was that they had used plants--as in spies, not flora--to infiltrate the Brand. How else could a fortress like that have been overrun so quickly? The dead ain't exactly known for their organizational skills.

We rejoiced when the Stone Show returned. We drank to Mother Margaret's death, live on video, and at the hands of her own husband. And we drank to the resulting collapse of the Left Hand Cult. We laughed at the irony that the Stone Show was now being broadcast from the Government's official bunker. If you know anything about the Stone Show's history with the FCC, you'd understand how that was like Superman and Lex Luther moving in together. Martin's absence from the show was hard to ignore, but we, at least, held out hope that he was still alive somewhere.

Then, one morning, we're listening over breakfast. They were running a segment on people's daily routines. Some guy named Caleb Kaiser calls in from Upper Marlboro, Maryland. Says he starts every morning by listening to our song *"Ride the Serpentine"* in honor of his wife Thana, our "number one fan," who died 6-months-ago. He goes into their story. They met at a concert during the *Ride the Serpentine* Tour. Love at first sight. Married for 17 years. One child; a son, Liam. Nine-years-old. Dead. The caller choked up at that point. Deadfucks, I assumed.

"My Thana," he goes. "She was never the same after the death of our son. It broke her. She regressed to a happier time in her life to cope with it. Started dressing like she did when we first met. She was a groupie for Serpentine at the time. Real diehard. Followed them all over the country. She would go around calling the lead singer Graeme Gunz her husband. She never even met the guy. That was actually a point of contention during the first few years of our marriage."

The caller stopped, blew out some air. You could hear the emotion in his breath. I wanted to yell at him to continue, but my head was spinning from his story, mainly the description of his wife, Thana. I suddenly felt cold. Goosebumps. I look over at Gramps. He was white as a ghost—no pun intended.

"What I wouldn't give to have her back," the caller continued. "She had gotten this idea in her head that she was missing the concert in Baltimore. The one where we first met. She would take one of the cars and run. We had to start restraining her. It was awful. She begged me to loosen her restraints. She said they hurt her wrists. I didn't want to, but she begged me. You see. She was in such pain. I couldn't bear to see her like that. So I did what she asked..."

He paused. No exhale this time. Just dead air.

"She got out that night," he could hardly say the words. "We found her car two days later. It was on its roof, half-submerged on the bank of Palmer Lake."

The caller descends into full-on weeping. And that becomes the background noise for the biggest "Holy Shit" moment this side of finding out that deadfucks were real.

Gramps blew chunks all over the table. Holly blew chunks at the sight and smell of Gramps' half-digested breakfast. I would've laughed if I wasn't so fucking shell-shocked. We went through the rest of the day on auto-pilot, avoiding eye contact and moving around the Grotto like strangers who shared a dark secret. I finally had enough and suggested the one thing that I knew would get our minds off this shit.

"Let's jam."

It took a little coaxing, but we got a good session in. I let the guys in on the lyrics I wrote about our number one fan. Now I had a title, Thana, and a story to reference from. It didn't take long for a song to materialize. I approached it from the angle of unrequited love and how far we'll go to obtain the object of our undying affection. I wrote a version where she got what she wanted. Gramps wasn't the biggest fan, but he understood the process.

The next day on the Stone Show, a woman named Janice calls in with a few words of support for "that poor man from yesterday's show who lost his wife and son." She goes on to describe how *"Ride the Serpentine"* has special meaning to her as well. She credits the song with giving her strength when she's feeling overwhelmed and ready to throw in the towel.

Imagine that. I never saw *Ride* as an inspirational tune. To me it's just the manifestation of the wave of "Fuck Yeah!" I was riding when I wrote the damn thing. It was '87, I think. Right around the time when we graduated from famous to God-like status. Back when my head was the size of a frickin' bowling ball. I defy anyone to live through that shit without it going to your head a little.

On the Stone Show, co-host Raven and Janice share legendary rock anecdotes. They name-drop Serpentine in the same breath as the Stones, the Who, Zeppelin, Guns n' Roses, Metallica, as groups that changed the game. They call Gramps the slithery personification of Rock 'n' Roll and they call me a bonafide Guitar God. I can live with that. They even throw Holly a bone when one of the behind-the-scenes guys goes into this rant about how it must suck to be the drummer in a successful rock group. "You're like window dressing," he goes. "...an afterthought..." They debate the subject for a while.

The Stone Show opens with the song the next day. Somehow it just fits. They open the show with it from then on. I don't think I've ever felt more proud of one of my babies.

Raven jokes about a lawsuit since they hadn't officially gotten permission to use the song.

Me and the guys decide to prank the show. What better way to let everyone know that we're still alive. Holly calls in as our former attorney Ira Levinthal. Good old Ira. Always

49

wondered what happened to him. He was such a pussy that it couldn't have been good.

"It's my intention to serve you with a Cease and Desist order unless my clients are paid for the use of their song," Holly—as Ira—says to Raven on the air. She catches him off-guard when she plays along with the joke. Holly runs out of legal mumbo-jumbo and let's the cat out of the bag.

Raven seems genuinely happy to hear from us. We spend the next hour and seventeen minutes telling our story post 9/6, affectionately remembering Martin Stone, and waxing philosophical about the power of music.

We thank the callers and fans, and the show for giving them a voice. We end the call with an acoustic rendition of "Ride."

A week later, we get an invite to the Weather from the President, himself. He wanted us to take part in the telethon. Kinda scary that Dick "Speaker of the House" Woellper is the guy currently calling the shots. You remember Dick. Slimy, weak-jawed Bible-thumper who cheated on his wife with his 16-year-old babysitter. Looks like Mr. Furley on a four-day-binge. That's a *Three's Company* reference for all you youngsters.

It always seemed like somebody was looking out for ole Dick. The media shit-storm over "Babysitter-gate" had just started to kick up when the deadfucks rained on everyone's parade. Then we lost the President and Vice President when Marine One disappeared from radar somewhere over the Atlantic a few months ago. Some people say it was an outbreak on board. Some say it was hijacked.

Raven makes this big announcement about us joining the telethon. "Serpentine's Coming!" she goes with all the fanfare of an upcoming World Tour. Someone on the staff floats the idea of Serpentine as the Stone Show's house band. The calls start rolling in. Before you know it, the thing takes on a life of its own.

A few days later, Caleb Kaiser calls in to express his joy over us coming aboard as the house band. Then the bastard completely hijacks the moment with some reoccurring dream where his dead wife Thana begs him to take her to the show in Baltimore—the same one she was headed to when she crashed. Bastard had everyone in tears.

Then, Holly calls the show—behind our backs--and gets in on the lovefest. He essentially volunteers us to perform at some memorial service Caleb and his people had put together for what would have been his and Thana's 18th wedding anniversary. "We pass right through Upper Marlboro on our way to the Weather," Holly goes. Like that means something…

That would be Upper Marlboro, Maryland, by the way. Home of the legendary Great Plains Amusement Park. I'd never heard of it either, but apparently it was some kinda big deal back in the day. Nowadays it's where Caleb Kaiser and his group live, in the utility tunnels underneath the main park.

Me and Gramps were pissed. You see, Holly had been sittin' on a few theories about our number one fan and how we might get rid of her. Caleb's dream was just the piece to the puzzle that he was looking for.

"It all makes since now," Holly directs his explanation at Gramps mostly. "We give her what she wants. *That's* how we end it."

I do the same. "I seem to remember the bitch trying to feed Gramps to one-a-*them.*" *Them* being deadfucks.

He comes back with. "How do we know she wasn't just trying to turn him?"

"Oh. That's okay, then," I joke.

I see Gramps' eyes light up. And I think; "*Fuck! He's got 'em!*" Then Holly comes in for the kill.

"Just think about it for a minute…" he goes. "If Thana can't have her concert, then maybe having Gramps to herself is the next best thing." He takes a dramatic pause. "So, we go there and give her a concert. Isn't that how these stories usually work? The spirit can't rest until some wrong is made right… Some unfinished business attended to… It usually stops when that *thing* is resolved. Right?"

"Forget all this bullshit about Thana," I say. "We've been invited to the safest place on Earth to essentially help heal the world through music—as Hellishly corny as that sounds. And you wanna risk all that to go on some Scooby-frickin'-Doo adventure?"

"Helloooo!" Holly goes. "We're living in a Scooby-frickin'-Doo adventure."

"Yeah. But this ain't Mr. Wickles or fucking… Hank from Gold City that we're dealing with here." A Miner 49er reference for ya. I've closed out many-a-nights drunk off my ass and tripping balls on the couch with Scooby and the gang. I preferred the old shit. Before Scrappy and all the guest stars. Frickin' Harlem Globetrotters, for fuck sakes…

Gramps cuts in, "I like it."

I give him a "Wha…" half-thinking he's referring to our Scooby Doo riff.

"I like where Holly's going with this," he says.

Which lights a fire under Holly's ass…

"It makes sense. Right?" Holly goes. "All those old ghost stories seem to follow a similar pattern. What's to say they're not based on some real shit? Aren't most cultural myths?"

I'll admit, he got me thinking, but I still felt like it was a leap… and an overall bad-fucking- idea. I mean… when you've got a ticket to the big show, you don't stop off at Open Mic Night at Joe's Corner Tavern on the way. Ok. Maybe that was a bad analogy, but you get my drift.

To seal the deal, the sneaky fuck appeals to Gramps' filmmaking obsession. "You can film the whole thing as part of the documentary," he goes. "Bing. Bang. Boom."

"Bing. Bang. Boom," was Holy's go-to-closer back in the old days. I thought he'd outgrown it. Apparently I was wrong.

We went back and forth for awhile. By the end of it, Gramps was all in and I was out-voted 2-to-1.

Episode #2:
She's Your No #1 Fan

<u>Video (Canon Vixia HF HD Camera)</u>

Interior of van / Scenery outside windows

May 17th, 10:05am

An impromptu jam session, already in progress. Guns and Roses' "Sweet Child of Mine," blaring from the speakers. Hollister pounds out a beat on the steering wheel. Graeme does his Serpentine dance in the passenger seat as he sings along with Axl Rose. Jules on acoustic guitar in the back seat.

Jules (V.O.): People used to say that Gramps stole his moves from Axl. Maybe that was true in the beginning, when we competitors on the Hollywood club scene. At some point, though, you've gotta give it up to Gramps for taking that shit to the next level. The way that boy moves makes Axl's swaying look like some middle-aged, suburban dad getting his groove on at his daughter's wedding reception.

Hollister stops drumming. His body stiffens. Jules zeros in on Hollister. His fingers become less dexterous. He finally stops playing. Graeme is still lost in the lyrics. Eyes squeezed shut. Seated Serpentine dance.

Hollister turns the music off and listens over Graeme's singing.

Jules (to Hollister): What is it?

Hollister shakes his head, "I dunno," while reaching into the center console for his handgun.

Hollister: Gunshots, maybe...

The Frame freezes as Hollister casts a concerned gaze out

the window in the direction of the familiar sound. Graeme in mid-Serpentine dance. The dawning of surprise colors his face. Jules shooting daggers at Hollister, "I told you so."

Jules (V.O.): This is like the part in *The Dukes of Hazzard* where Waylon Jennings comments on just how fucked "Them Duke Boys" are. Yee Haw!

The Frame resumes.

Graeme (to Hollister): Gunshots?

Hollister presses a button. The driver-and-passenger-side-windows slide shut. Graeme produces a firearm from the glovebox and holds it close. Jules unstraps his guitar and replaces it with an automatic weapon.

Outside, a narrow road hugged by ranch-style homes and businesses, vacant and vandalized several times over. A major intersection up ahead. A large sign directs amusement park visitors to the right.

"WELCOME TO UPPER MARLBORO, HOME OF THE WORLD FAMOUS GREAT PLAINS AMUSEMENT PARK"

Hollister reduces speed and sets his eyes on scan. He points to the right.

Hollister (re: gunshots): I'm pretty sure they came from that direction.

Jules: Of course they did.

Hollister: Maybe it's some kinda welcome.

Graeme casts a cynical glare at the camera.

Hollister: I'm just saying... Could be a million reasons. No need to jump to conclusions.

Graeme leans closer to the window and looks past his faint reflection, at the scenery on the other side.

Hollister: Stay sharp, just the same.

Jules: Way ahead-a-you on that one.

The van turns right at the intersection and creeps a quarter of a mile down a massive driveway that leads to the amusement park. The driveway eventually cuts through an overgrown picnic area hidden beneath layers of neglect. Park benches and group canopy areas break the surface of refuse. Several signs along the way convey an African motif with directional markers in the form of tribal spears pointing straight ahead. Words floating above the markers, "Entrance to Main Park."

Up ahead, a massive archway of man-made vines twisting and intertwined. "Great Plains Amusement Park," etched in a colorful, safari-style font into the façade. "A Tocsek Brothers Company," in smaller white letters beneath it.

The archway stands before a vast parking lot. A handful of abandoned vehicles. Tall light-posts wearing lettered, parking placards like rectangular bow-ties. Cameras mounted on the light-post. Wind-scattered refuse. A few bodies, twice dead. A haphazard trail cut into the refuse. An 18-wheeler lay on its side at the end of the trail. Rear door left wide open. Skid marks tell the story of a sharp turn taken too fast. A few undead wander away from the truck toward a much larger crowd of, at least, 100 in front of the amusement park proper, some 50-feet away. A small feeding frenzy by the truck's front tire. A pair of freshly-clothed legs jutting out from the pulsating mound of undead. The swarm of clawing, tearing hands make the legs appear to kick. A spent Russian RPG-27 lay just outside the mound. A weathered satchel nearby, its contents spilled out onto the ground as if it was flung away in haste.

Several trailers parked tail-to-tip block the entrance to the park. A large hole blown in the side of one of the trailers.

Undead climbing through. More undead clawing at their backs. Two men, positioned on top of the trailers, use handguns to thin the herd one-by-one. They run out of bullets and resort to a pair of Tee-ball bats, leaning precariously over the edges of the trailers and taking wild swings that mostly miss their targets.

Jules (re: undead): Welcome to the Terrordome, bitches!

Graeme (re: undead): You know. I actually convinced myself that we were done with this kind of shit.

Jules: Yet here we are again, brother.

Hollister: Well. We can't just leave 'em hanging.

Silence…

Hollister: *I SAID*: 'We can't just leave them hanging?'

Jules: Shit, Holly! Ain't like we haven't done it before. And over way less than this. Must be 100-a-those fuckers out there.

Hollister: One-hundred and sixty-three, actually.

Jules (V.O.): Holly and his fucking mathematical brain.

Graeme (concerned): Maybe this wasn't such a good idea, Holly.

Jules: Ya think?!

Hollister: I can't believe what I'm hearing from you two.

Jules: I've made no secret about my feelings on this.

Hollister (to Jules): What happened to all that horseshit about a higher calling? "Bigger than the hit records and awards. Bigger than the all the money and the pussy." Because I was right there with you when you were preachin' that shit.

(to Graeme) Don't act like you weren't, too?

Graeme makes a face at being called out.

Jules (V.O.): The son-of-a-bitch reaches back to one of my brief stints as Captain Optimism.

Hollister (to Jules): So, was that all just horseshit?

Jules: That was before you volunteered us for this gig.

Hollister: Like it or not, everything changed the moment Caleb Kaiser called into the Stone Show. Now, we're part of the official narrative, permanently woven into the zeitgeist of this new world that *WE* will help conquer. They'll write about us in history books. Children will tell stories about us. They'll teach our music in schools. And *THIS* is how we repay the guy who set all that in motion? By bailing on him in a time of crisis? A week ago you were talkin' about blowing the dude.

Jules: Whoa! Let's not get crazy. It was a joke.

Hollister: We're talking two days, tops, guys. We enjoy a little hospitality, then we rock the balls off this place to kick-start our comeback. You can't tell me that either of you chumps aren't sportin' wood at the thought of tearing through our old setlist.

Jules (V.O.): Caleb Kaiser requested that we do the setlist from our *"Ride the Serpentine"* Tour.

Graeme: I hear you, Holly, but we don't know what we're walking into here. I think it's a safe bet that that big rig came full of deadfucks; the same ones that are trying to get through the hole in the side of that trailer, which I'm guessing wasn't put there by accident.

Jules: Looks like the fucknut who did it went and got himself killed.

Graeme: How do we know he wasn't alone? And even if he

was, we don't know anything about anything. Maybe this Kaiser dude is another Zamora-type, and he deserved this shit. Maybe we're rolling right into the lion's den.

Jules: He's got a point, Holly. Fact is… something pissed off that poor shithead enough to make him go through the trouble of finding a rig that still had gas in the tank, or if it didn't, finding gas, wrangling all those deadfucks into the back of thing, and driving it over here. That's enough to give me concern. I'm thinking of the bigger picture here. How the Hell're we gonna save the world if we never even make it to the Promised Land in the first place?

Hollister takes a breath, weighs their options.

A female voice comes over the CB radio. Traces of a South American Accent.

Female Voice (over radio): You. In the black van. If you're part-a-this, then you can rest assured that we will hunt you down and…

A strangely affected male voice interrupts. Undecipherable whispering on the other end.

The boys look at each other. Hollister picks up the hand-held.

Hollister (into hand-held): To whom am I speaking? Over.

Male voice (over radio, excited): Boys! Wow! You're really here? So glad you could make it. This is Caleb Kaiser speaking. You'll have to excuse my head-of-security. We're in a bit of a jam, as you can see. We could certainly use your help. Over.

Jules (V.O.): It didn't sound like the same guy who called into the Stone Show a week-and-a-half ago. The tone and timbre were there, but the delivery was like somebody randomly switching channels between *Alvin and the Chipmunks* and Snuffleupagus from *Sesame Street*.

Hollister (into hand-held): What seems to be the problem? Over.

Graeme (whispers to Hollister): I think it's kinda obvious.

Caleb (over radio): It's not as bad as it looks. Just a disgruntled former member looking for some payback for being voted out. Caught us with our pants down, I guess you could say. We're extremely low on firearms and ammo. You help us out and I'll make it worth your while. Food. Supplies. Lodging. Whatever you boys need. Over.

Hollister lowers the hand-held, turns to the others.

Hollister (to Jules and Graeme): I guess that solves our problem for us, huh?

Jules: Fuck me, dude! That *disgruntled former member* could have a friend who's out there waiting to pick us off.

Hollister points at the two men atop the trailers.

Hollister: Why aren't they picking them off, then?

Caleb (over radio): You still there? I say, we could really use your help.

A moment of introspection. Roving glances. Jules exhales loudly.

Jules: It's gonna eat up a shitload of ammo.

Hollister: We don't have to waste all of 'em. Just take out the first tier. Use it to make a statement. Make 'em think twice. Then we go in there and we give that spooky bitch the show to die for. Literally!

Hollister extends his arm—palm down, fingers flexed—and lets it hover in the space between his bandmates.

Hollister: Now... Who's with me?!

Graeme is first to acquiesce. As he places his hand on top of Hollister's...

Graeme: Since you put it that way...

All eyes on Jules now... He hesitates before reluctantly placing his hand on top of Graeme's.

Jules: Just for the record, I'm doing this under protest.

Hollister: Oh... keep your skirt on, Julie. Sheesh. And I thought I was supposed to be Mr. Buzzkill.

Graeme chuckles.

Jules: You ARE.

Hollister: Not this time, apparently.

A breathy simper from Jules.

Hollister: We'll be fine.

Jules: Fine. Yeah...

Hollister nods at the cello case propped against the rear doors.

Hollister: Speaking of making a statement...

Video (Great Plains CCTV Cam – Various)

Parking lot / Main Entrance

The black Ford Sportsmobile peels off and accelerates, tires kicking up smoke. It passes under the massive archway and continues forward, carving a path through the refuse-strewn parking lot, toward the undead converged at the entrance. Brakes squeal as the van spins out and comes to rest with its back to the entrance, 50-feet away.

Dim-witted caution from some of the undead. The others continue to work toward their initial goal.

The shriek of audio feedback comes through the van's megaphones... Guitar chords, like someone warming up.

Graeme (via megaphone): Undead shitheads of Great Plains! This one here goes out to all our warm-blooded brothers and sisters who want nothing more than for you dried-up, pea-brain, pieces-of-shit to take your rotten, stinkin', flesh-eating asses right back to the Hell that spawned you. So... Without further adieu, I give you the uncanny, inhuman guitar stylings of the baddest motherfucker to ever pick up an axe. My right hand man! My brother from another mother! The axeman cometh, in the fucking flesh! The one! The only! JULES-MOTHER-FUCKING-YEAGERRRRR!

The van's rear doors fly open. Jules leaps down from inside, GiGi 2.0 strapped across his torso. A belt of machine-gun bullets fed into her side. It drags on the ground behind him.

Jules swings his arm in a wide arc and comes down hard across the guitar strings. An aggressive chord leads off an extended, fast-fingered solo. Bullets fly from the headstock as Jules' fingers dance, his other hand stroking the neck.

The men atop the trailers dive for cover as Jules sinks deeper into trance-like communion with the guitar Gods. His fingers move with inhuman dexterity and GiGi 2.0 wails accordingly. His hips gyrate and thrust. His face twists into a mask of deep concentration, narrowed eyes locked on his multi-limbed, pulsating target up ahead. His head nods as if to acknowledge the surge of pure adrenaline.

Jules (V.O.): The world looked different whenever I held Gigi in my arms. She took me to a place where all that mattered was the music. Where slices of pure fucking sonic gold are born from the cosmic slop. This one here's something new I wrote; a little nod to Eddie's Van Halen's "Eruption" with a Jules Yeager twist that I call "Sonic Stomp."

Lead-laced chords inspire a mosh-pit of stiff-jointed, brain-bursting vigor as bullets tear through the undead mass. The remaining undead abandon their attempt to gain entry into the amusement park. Some cower from the onslaught of bullets while others just stand there casting eyes full of puzzlement and sedated fear on the man with the machine-gun-guitar.

Jules is in the zone, at a place where his actions are not his own, but those of a higher power speaking through him. And he doesn't appear to be stopping anytime soon.

VIDEO (Great Plains CCTV Cam – Various / Canon Vixia HF HD Camera – Graeme's POV)

Amusement Park

A colorful maze of rides, game-tents, and concession booths muted by exposure to the elements. Larger structures loom in the background. Ferris wheel. Roller Coasters. Surreal, carny-style murals for featured attractions. Goofy human-like caricatures lunging from raised signage. Exaggerated glee weathered down to lunatic grimaces. Fully realized statues, equally weathered; an angry sea-serpent in pursuit of a mermaid atop the Log Plume. A winged demon with swirling eyes peeking over the roof of the haunted house. Clothed animals stuck in welcoming poses guide visitors to the children's area.

Caleb Kaiser (Late 30s) leads the way on a pre-determined route meant to conceal the small group's movement from the dead loitering at the PVC coated, wire-mesh fencing that surrounds the park. A medley of concerned grunts and dry-throated wailing pours from a quartet of megaphones mounted atop tall wooden poles placed along the park's perimeter.

Caleb conveys a sensible vibe and an understated authority wrapped in a cloak of functional drug addiction. His clothing (slacks, a button-down, and a sensible blazer with dark-colored elbow patches) suggests that he still puts some thought into what he wears, even if it looks thrice slept-in. A *cyclone of sagging, slightly darkened skin beneath his eyes suggests lack of sleep.*

Jules and Hollister follow closely behind Caleb. Graeme in back holding the Vixia to his eye. A heavily-armed, tightly wound Latina (Valentina "Tina" Escalante, 40s) trails the group. She is Caleb's head of security.

A silent dialogue between Graeme, Jules, and Hollister as they take in the surreal atmosphere. Graeme's roving POV eventually lands on Tina. She returns a defiant glare, eyes, like Caleb's, resting atop a cyclonic sag of slightly darkened skin. It's obvious that she doesn't like being on camera.

Tina Escalante is slight in stature. All of five feet tall with a pinched face and dressed like an urban guerilla on extended holiday. A Russian AK 101 strapped to her back. She looks like the physical manifestation of the aggressive female voice from the CB radio.

Jules (V.O.): It's funny how living-death and neglect can turn a once happy place into Satan's bad acid trip. And how witnessing the impossible on a daily basis opens your mind to silly thoughts about statues coming to life and inflicting bodily harm or swallowing you whole. But dammit if I didn't think just that as we walked the gauntlet of oversized smiles and scowls baring down from every direction. Caleb Kaiser was running in a different gear from the guy who called into the Stone Show. If I was to make an educated guess, I'd say he was riding a rollercoaster of uppers and downers. Not a good mix. Somebody was definitely over-medicating this guy. Or he was doing it himself.

I could see the man underneath all that; the sort of a goody-two-shoes, Christian alpha-male. Probably a closet fan until his wife brought it out into the open. And I could understand why someone, in his situation--losing his wife and kid like that, and in such a short time-frame--would want to just check out, especially on the eve of what would've been his 18th anniversary.
You like how I did that? How I just reasoned away all my

64

concerns about the guy? I'm gettin' pretty good at that.

Tina Escalante was like a powder keg of primal, Earthy appeal, South American-style. Colombia, I'm guessing from the accent. She had a face like an upside-down triangle, all cheekbones, and big, brown eyes, and bronze skin, and jet-black hair that never seemed to move from in front of her right eye. She also had a permanent resting—"I'll cut your nuts off,"—face that would make most guys think twice about approaching her. In that respect, she was typical for a head-of-security type. She was all, "No cameras," when we first came in. Caleb put the kibosh on that noise with some speech about their place is "this historic event," and the magic of happenstance. "Don't you feel it?" he goes. Sounded like he'd been smoking the same shit as Holly.

The two jokers on top of the trailers out front were Tina E's twin brothers Frick and Frack aka Christian and Mateo. Neither of them wanted to appear on camera. "This ain't entertainment to us," they go. Their loss. Aside from the family resemblance to Tina E., they were just a pair of forgettable, humorless wannabe hard-asses. The world is full of 'em these days.

Caleb rambles like a sunny-side-up tour guide/game show host. He gives us a history lesson that I barely listen to. Too much to see. Holly does most of the legwork in the ice-breaking department while me and Gramps gawk like a pair of tourists.

I check back into the conversation when Caleb thanks us for intervening at the front gate, "on behalf of the residents here at Great Plains."

Trying to keep things light, as usual, I jump on the opportunity to stick it to Holly.

Jules: Well... we couldn't just leave you hanging.

Jules slides Holly a shit-eating grin.

Holly throws back a scowl.

Caleb: One thing's for sure; you boys sure haven't forgotten how to make an entrance. No sir.

Caleb addresses the boys over his shoulders, rambling in a rasped whisper. He occasionally turns around and walks backward. His eyes dart, stealing glances at Tina throughout the conversation, like a man seeking approval.

Jules: Guess I got a little carried away out there.

Hollister (annoyed): Ya think?

Jules (to Hollister): You *said* to make a statement.

Hollister: Not at the expense of the fucking battery.

Jules: Well. How was I supposed to kno…?

Tina: (interrupts): Keep your voices down.

Jules throws his hands up in surrender and then gestures as if zipping his lips.

Caleb (to Hollister): What's that you're driving?

Hollister: It's just a tricked out Ford Sportsmobile.

Caleb: Looks like you might be safer in that thing than here with us. I'm kidding, of course. Pretty impressive piece of machinery, though. What's it? Military?

Hollister: No. Nothing like that. Its bark is much worse than its bite. Trust me.

Caleb: How'd you come across it?

Awkward silence…

Caleb: Yeah. Well… I'm sure we can find a battery for you in one of the vehicles out back. No sweat. Easy Peezy.

Hollister: That'd be great. Thanks.

Caleb: Don't mention it. Not at all.

Graeme directs Caleb's attention to the voices pouring from the megaphones.

Graeme (to Caleb): Some kinda deterrent?

Caleb animates without warning.

Caleb: DING! DING! DING! You-are-correct, sir!

Tina (to Caleb): SHHHHHH!

Caleb straightens up and proceeds as if the outburst never happened.

Caleb (to Graeme): It's not foolproof, but it's a fairly effective deterrent. You see, the smarter ones react with reverence, even fear, in some cases, to certain vocalizations. The others react to the smart ones' apprehension. Okay... So, it becomes less effective once they get riled up, as you saw earlier. But it blows the pants off the gunfire medley we were using up to that point, which they start to get used to when you're essentially dealing with the same crowd all the time.

Jules: Gunfire medley.... I like that. Sounds like something we shoulda put out in the '80s.

Caleb: Apparently these particular vocalizations tap into some base instinct for self- preservation or something intelligent sounding like that. Doc Mokae's responsible for all that. It's his thing. He was one of Dr. Hammond's people, you know. You remember Dr. Hammond. Right? From the Stone Show? Doc Mokae was part of the team that came up with that microchip. The one that was supposed to control the dead. Remember that? Of course you remember.

Jules perks up.

Jules: Yeah! We know Dr. Hammond. I mean... we don't know him, know him. But we heard the interview.

Jules (V.O.): For all you non-Stone-Show-fans out there, Dr. Franklin Hammond was this big-shot neurologist famous for his cutting-edge research into implanting microchips in the brain as a way of treating all kinds-a-conditions. His interview was one of the high points of the show. They took him and his people in at the Weather after their settlement in Downingtown, Pa was raided by the Left Hand. Now they work for Uncle Sam. Bet *they* didn't stop off on the way to do... surgeries for charity or something.

Jules: No offense, but shouldn't Dr. Moe-kabe, is it, be with Hammond and his people at the Weather?

Caleb: None taken. Not at all. And it's pronounced Moe-kay. Moe...Kay... It's African. Ghanaian, I believe. That's where he's from. You can ask him all about it when you meet him a little later.

Caleb guides the boys to a windowless steel door behind a concession booth marked "Utilidor Entrance - Employees Only."

Caleb: This way. This way...

VIDEO (Great Plains CCTV Cam – Various / Canon Vixia HF HD Cam – Graeme's POV)

Concrete Corridor

We move down a ramp into a long tunnel. A surf-rock serenade pours from the PA system. Concrete walls. A ceiling of blue piping extends as far as the eyes can see. The mother of all pipes hugs the left wall. A few rooms interrupt the flow on that side. Great Plains Amusement Park Signage on the doors. The park logo emblazoned on the side of several golf carts parked along the opposite wall. Intersecting corridors at the far end, some 50-feet away. A golf cart parked at the opening of the left corridor.

Caleb Kaiser, the boys, and Tina Escalante are walking in the same formation as before.

Jules is preoccupied with the layout of the place and by the music pouring from the PA.

Jules (V.O.): There's a mental checklist you run through when you come to these places.

• Does it have adequate protection?
A. From the dead *and* the living
B. From the elements

• What's the tone of leadership/populace?
• What's the food situation?

If you were able to get down to superficial things…

• Quality of life (safe access to the outside world/general distractions from confinement)
• Comfortable beds.
• Doable chicks.

…then you were probably in a decent place.
The verdict was still out on Great Plains. The image of our weapons sitting in a safe, in the guard station, flashes across my mind and I catch a wave of vulnerability. We were asked to leave them there when we first came in. It's a pretty common practice among settlements.

I could see how someone could lose it down here in what is essentially a network of windowless, concrete corridors, and pipes of various sizes painted a weird shade of blue. Somewhere between lapis and sky. Compliments of the Pantone Formula Guide. You'll read just about anything when you've got nothing but time on your hands.

Jules looks into the camera and makes a face at the music pouring from the speakers.

I got a kick out of the Serpentine retrospective coming over the PA system, even if it was currently on my least favorite album from our catalogue.

Graeme (to Caleb, re: music): Sanguine Surf. Huh?

Caleb: It's one of my all-time faves.

A collective groan from the boys.

Caleb: What's wrong?

Graeme: A lot of bad memories associated with that album.

They pass a large open space on the right marked Cafeteria. Several long, cafeteria-style tables inside. An unmanned service counter. A food warming station under a glass canopy. Empty.

Caleb's mood changes without warning. He stands in the doorway of the cafeteria bursting with manic enthusiasm.

Caleb: Our cafeteria... Compliments of the Great Plains Utilidor System. Management really went all out when they put this place together. Cafeteria. Gym. Living quarters. An infirmary that would rival a small town hospital. That's what sold Doc Mokae on the place.

Jules: I'm sure it had nothing at all to do with his not wanting to get eaten or shot by some fucknut out in the shit.

Caleb: There's that...

Caleb's weird enthusiasm vanishes as quickly as it appeared. Disappointment in its place.

Caleb: Okay wait... Really? I mean... Really? Sanguine Surf? That movie was like a cultural phenomenon. In large part because of the soundtrack.

It takes the boys a moment to catch up.

Jules: Maybe so. But we were knee deep in it, at that point. I'm surprised we managed to get anything done.

A confused look from Caleb.

Jules: Nose Candy. Blow. Yayo. China white. Snow. Sneeze. Dust. Toot. Big rush...

Hollister (interrupts): I think he gets the picture.

Jules: We didn't even wanna do the thing, at first. Vampire surfers for fuck sakes. It was just supposed to be a minor part so Gramps could get his feet wet as an *AK-TOR*. But then they threw a shitload of money at us to do the music. So we just put our minds on autopilot and channeled Dick Dale meets Goblin.

Caleb: Who, the Hell, is Goblin?

Jules shudders.

Jules: Now, that's blasphemy, right there. I'm assuming you're not a fan of '80s Italian Horror.

Caleb: I didn't even know that was a thing.

Jules shakes his head.

Jules: Remind me to school you one of these days.

Caleb: I'll put it on my list.

A few seconds pass...

Graeme: So, my girl, at the time—back when we did *Sanguine Surf*—she kept pushing me to get into acting.

Jules: The British chick. Right?

Graeme: Sophia

Jules: The one with the droopy face.

Graeme: Fuck you, man! She was better than that skank you were running around with.

Jules: Whoa! Down boy! I didn't say she wasn't hot. I said she had a droopy face. And my girl wasn't a skank. She was a junkie. There's a difference.

Graeme smiles, shakes his head.

Graeme (with affection): Asshole.

Hollister: Guys!

Caleb is amused by their interaction.

Caleb (to Graeme): Well. If it's any consolation, I thought you rocked in that movie.

Graeme: Thanks, man. It turned out better than we all thought. The album, too. We definitely pulled that one out of our asses, though.

Jules: Amen to that shit.

Caleb gazes into the middle distance and channels Artie Johnson from Laugh In.

Caleb: Very interesting…

Jules (V.O.): I can see that this guy was a genuine fan. By genuine, I mean "in love with a romanticized version of us," manufactured by record company A&Rs and the press. It was an image that we could never live up to in person. Especially now. Could be a problem down the road. Another bullet point for the old mental notes.

Holly breaks into interrogation mode while I wrestle with endless possibilities.

Hollister (to Caleb): So, you and your people been here since the beginning, huh?

Caleb's face jumps affable.

Caleb: That's right... That's right... Originally, our group was made up of park employees and some guests who were here when the shit hit the fan. We picked up a few along the way. Lost a few more. You boys know how it is. Of course you do.

Caleb stops, suddenly enchanted by the sexy-cool guitar solo oozing from the PA. He closes his eyes...

Caleb: Wait... Wait... I *looove* this part.

...and falls deep into an air-guitar trance. He sways, and thrashes, and gyrates in an astute homage to Jules shredding on his axe.

Tina intercepts Hollister's attempt to regain Caleb's attention, and then shakes her head, "No."

Tina (whispers, to Hollister): Just let it play itself out.

One minute and fifteen seconds later...

Caleb emerges from his trance, all smiles.

Caleb (to Jules): Man-o-man! I don't know how you did it, but that, right there, is pure magic.

Jules is disarmed by Caleb's enthusiasm. He flashes a self-congratulatory smile.

Jules: Well... You know... The best ones always come when you least...

Daggers of cynicism from Graeme and Hollister snatch away Jules' smile, and his acceptance speech.

Jules (embarrassed, to Caleb): Thanks.

Afterward, Caleb searches the air for his last, pre-guitar-solo thought...

Tina (to Caleb): You were telling them about this place...

A spark of memory...

Caleb (to the boys): You see... It wasn't my intention to run things, but the people took a vote early on and here I am. I was working as head-of-security for the park when it all went down. My background is in law-enforcement; hostage-negotiation, specifically. Did 15-years with the Baltimore PD before I got burned-out. So, I guess it makes sense when you look at it that way. Lucky me. Right?

Hollister: No offense, but that whole thing at the front gate looked far too complicated for a pissed off former resident to pull off.

Caleb stops walking just short of the intersecting corridor. A golf cart parked at a cockeyed angle a few feet away. Weighty contemplation colors Caleb's expression. His eyes dart. Tina stiffens, seemingly distressed by his reaction.

Curious glances pass between the boys.

Caleb exhales.

Caleb: About that... I haven't been completely honest...

Jules chafes at Caleb's revelation.

Jules: Here we go...

Hollister: Jules!

Caleb: The man behind that... *situation* out front... Bridger was his name. Trent Bridger. He was, in fact, a former resident here. Yep. Fraid so... Never did like the guy, as a matter of fact. Too hard to get along with. And I get along with everyone. It's like my father used to say...

Tina (interrupts, to Caleb): Stay on topic.

Caleb takes a moment to stifle his annoyance with Tina, and then picks up where he left off like nothing ever happened.

Caleb: We believe Bridger left with the intention of linking up with a bunch of knuckle-draggers who call themselves Swarm. They have a settlement—if you can call it that—a few miles northwest of here.

Tina: They'll take in any-old-cabrón over there. The crazier the better.

Caleb: Apparently not.

Tina sucks her teeth in disagreement. Caleb admonishes her with a hiss.

Caleb: My guess is Swarm turned Bridger away. Even *they* have standards, I suppose. Being the type of guy he was; incapable of accepting responsibility for his own actions, he lashed out at the people he blames for his current predicament. Us. What you boys witnessed was clearly a lone act of revenge. *Clearly*. Without a doubt... Mz. Escalante, here feels differently, however. She, and a few of the others here, think I'm being naïve. That I'm blinded by my devotion to my late wife's memorial concert. That I need an intervention.

Tina: I never said that! I just think you should consider the possibility that what happened out there was a trial run.

Caleb (to Tina): An unsuccessful one, if that's the case. But, I don't think it is. I mean... why now? We haven't heard as much as a peep from those troglodytes in months. (to boys) Their group has made a few attempts on this place in the past. All unsuccessful, I might add.

Tina: That was when we actually had weapons to fight them off.

Jules: That's just wonderful!

Caleb's demeanor changes, downshifting from affable hyper-drive to simmering irritation. His eyes become angry slits. He points them at Tina.

Hollister (to Caleb): Now look. We came here in good faith. If there's something going on that we should know about…

Caleb lowers his head and lets out an exasperated breath. He looks up a full 30-seconds-later in a calmer, more stable place.

Caleb (to boys): Please understand? Your being here means the world to me. More than that. I promise you there's nothing nefarious going on. My head-of-security tends to be overly cautious. And she has right to be. We lost most of our firepower when our armory burned down a few months ago. Unfortunate accident, it was. (to Tina) But it was just that. *An accident.* (to boys) As far as Bridger knew, we were able to salvage the guns. Like I said, I never trusted the guy. No one did. So, you see… Swarm has no way of knowing about the fire. (to Tina) If that's what you're insinuating.

Tina returns a face full of attitude and then walks around the boys and slides behind the wheel of the golf cart parked at the mouth of the corridor.

Caleb gets in beside her and gestures for the boys to follow.

VIDEO (Great Plains CCTV Cam – Various / Canon Vixia HF HD Camera – Graeme's POV)

Concrete Corridor

We are peering over the roof of the golf cart as it glides down another concrete corridor. More pipes. More rooms. Signage on walls and doors. Tina behind the wheel. Caleb riding shotgun, half-turned toward the rear where Jules and Hollister are squeezed side-by-side in the back seat. Graeme standing on a footrest right behind them, holding the Vixia. His crotch is in line with their eyes whenever they dare to turn and look back. Graeme occasionally leans to the left to see inside the cart.

Caleb in sunny-side-up, hyper-drive, rambles on…

Caleb (to Boys): You see… What you have with Swarm is a bunch of paranoid, intellectual infants posing as alpha males. The type of people who seek comfort in power and control. They're obsessed with securing some delusional position of power in the (mocking tone) *New World Order.* You know the type.

Jules: They're everywhere these days.

Graeme: Like roaches.

Caleb: Like roaches. Exactly right. The idiots have already made two failed attempts at raiding the vaccine caravans from the Weather, if that gives you an idea of the type of mentality we're dealing with.

Jules: How many we talking altogether?

Caleb: Our last count put their numbers at around 30.

Hollister: How is it that you know so much about these guys? If you don't mind my asking…

Caleb: Not at all. It's like I said… I spent 15-years in law-enforcement.

Hollister: What makes you so sure they won't attack again?

Caleb: Their focus seems to have shifted in the past couple of months. We have it on pretty good information that they mean to use a hostage they've recently acquired to negotiate some sort of deal with the government.

Jules: Holy Christ!!! And they knew we were coming here?!

Caleb: Those idiots are too busy fighting with each other to listen to the Stone Show.

Jules: You sure about that? Couple of rock legends in tight with uncle Sam might bring a good ransom. If you know what I mean.

Tina chuckles. Caleb gives her a scowling reprimand.

Caleb (to Jules): Positive. Whoever they've got, though... he's supposed to be some kind of bigshot.

Tina: Or she.

Caleb: I feel sorry for the poor bastard, whoever he (to Tina) *Or she...* is.

Jules (to Tina): Not a fan, I take it?

Tina doesn't respond. Smug satisfaction on her face.

The hum of the golf cart's engine scores a break in the conversation.

Graeme (to Caleb): Sooooo... About the concert...

Caleb: I can't wait for you boys to see what we've done with the planetarium.

Graeme leans to the side.

Graeme: Did you just say *planetarium*?

Caleb: That's where we're holding the concert. I tried to get everything as close to that night as possible. You remember? Friday, September 17th, 1987... Baltimore Civic Center... Ride the Serpentine Tour...

Jules: That's... kinda like asking a Catholic Priest if he

remembers all the…

Hollister nudges him.

Hollister: Sure. We remember.

Caleb: Of course you do… I was moonlighting as security for the Civic Center. Caught Thana and her girlfriend, Chloe trying to sneak backstage.

He looks over at Graeme.

Caleb: To see *you*… They had fake Press Badges. They had those little, mini-recorders that the reporters use. Sexy outfits hidden under baggy clothes and *smart-chick* glasses. They weren't messing around. No sir. I couldn't help but be impressed by their determination. And neither of 'em were bad on the eyes either. Especially Thana. Real Earthy, free-spirit type, she was. Her friend Chloe breaks down in tears and starts begging me not to get the police involved. Meanwhile Thana's giving it to me about how my spirit is corrupt and that's what's keeping me from being anything more than just a menial servant. I'm thinking; "The balls on this chick…" I loved it! I eventually said I'd let them go if she'd agree to go on a date with me. Chloe acts like I whipped out my Johnson or something. And in retrospect, I get it. So, I gave Thana my number and my word that I wouldn't tell the police. Then I let them go, not thinking that she'd ever call me.

Tina (to Caleb): You're drifting…

Caleb pauses, annoyed…

Caleb (to Tina): It's called riffing.

Tina: Not to mention, that story makes you sound like some kind of sexual predator every time you tell it.

Caleb (to Tina): A little creepy. Maybe. *Maybe*… But I'm redeemed by the fact that it worked out. (to the boys, re:

Tina): This coming from someone with the personality of a rock.

Graeme and Jules try not to laugh. No emotion from Tina.

Caleb: I've seen lizards with more personality.

Caleb mimics a lizard's blank stare.

Caleb: I've seen dead people with more personality.

He mimics an undead gaze.

Caleb: I've seen...

Tina (Calmly, to Caleb): Just get to the point. We're almost there.

Caleb looks ahead.

Caleb: Well look at that. We are... (to boys) So then, about a week later, I get a call. It's her. Thana. I almost shit my pants. To a guy like me... a good, Christian boy from the Midwest, Thana was larger than life. I couldn't fathom why she'd be into me. This cheerleader for alternative thinking. Reincarnation. Mental telepathy. The power of crystals... All this horseshit about out-of-body experiences and traveling to distant places simply by concentrating. And I'm over here trying to make sense of the father, the son, and the Holy Ghost. My brain's telling me to, "Head for zee hills," but my heart, not to mention my Johnson, is like, "Go for it! Screw your better judgement." It shouldn't have worked out, but somehow we connected over our love for you guys. In a way, you-all are responsible for bringing us together.

Jules: Glad we could be of service.

Caleb: Oh you've all been much more than that. Much more.

Jules is unsure how to respond.

Caleb: It was pretty rough in the beginning. I'll tell you what… You know how it is when you're young and you wear your heart on your sleeve. Over time we found a way to meet in the middle. She helped to open my mind to the idea that maybe there's something more to life as we know it. Our current situation is proof-enough of that. And I'd like to think I helped her come to a more… down-to-Earth view of the alternative.

The cart pulls over and stops in front of a pair of double doors marked "Planetarium."

Caleb: Well… Here we are. Mz. Escalante will show you around from here. She might not be the warmest body in the room, but she knows her stuff.

Caleb slides Tina a look, which she completely ignores.

Caleb: We'll get you all fed after you meet the team who put the show together. Later, I'd like to introduce you to Doc Mokae, if you don't mind. Won't take long. And I think you'll find his work fascinating. Especially if you're fans of Dr. Hammond. We can save the rest of the introductions until after the concert tomorrow. Let you boys rest up. We've got the C Wing all set up for you.

VIDEO (Great Plains CCTV Cam – Various / Canon Vixia HF HD Cam – Graeme's POV)

Planetarium

A large, circular room. Low light. Dark tones. An array of plush chairs arranged theatre-in-the-round style surrounds a circular stage sitting dead-center. A professional setup on top. Speakers. Amps. A full drum-kit. Guitars leaning on stands. A giant banner wrapped around the base of the stage reads: RIDE THE SERPENTINE TOUR 1987! Huge inflatable characters and creepy statues lifted from park attractions smile and glower at the empty chairs. Two men wrestle with a mess of wires jutting out from a panel in the stage-floor. Bad splices abound. They are part of a small

81

crew of individuals tending to the details. Sound. Lighting. Electrical. They turn toward the shrill noise from the door-hinge as Tina Escalante enters with the boys.

A sudden burst of light and sound from the dome walls/ ceiling. Clips of Serpentine, at their peak, explode across the screen. Concerts. Screaming fans. Lavish music videos.

The boys cower from the ambush of supersized memories. Graeme detaches the Vixia from his eye. His arm drops to his side as he and Jules are seduced by the image-storm. Dumb grins on both their faces as they come to a stand, heads cranked back to their shoulders. Hollister's response is more guarded, pensive.

Graeme (awestruck): Rock-and-fucking-*ROLL*!

Jules (V.O.): Don't be fooled by Holly's bullshit restraint. In that moment, I can safely say that Gramps spoke for all of us.

The screen goes black. A male voice comes across the speakers, "Screen works!"
Another male voice responds. "We saw!"

Jules (V.O.): Sensory overload like a motherfucker is what that was. I had to give it to them, though. They had a stage set-up that would rival some of the smaller venues we played. I could do without the creepy fucking statues. I got that they were paying homage to Clementine. Miss that girl. Clementine was to Serpentine what Eddie was to Iron Maiden. She was a badass, fully animatronic 14-foot serpentine dragon with laser-light eyes that breathed smoke and spit fire. A pair of snarling, bug-eyed, winged gargoyles standing in aggressive poses kinda missed the mark, in my opinion.

It's a lot to take in. Maybe too much. The whole thing left me with a headache and a hard-on for the good old days. You have to remember... Despite any misgivings I might have had about this place, my feet were still barely touching the ground from what amounted to sex with GiGi out in the parking lot. Then they hit us with this shit. The rocker in me wanted to jump on that stage and go balls-to-the-wall on that shiny fucking axe. The cynic in me joked that with my old knees, I shouldn't be jumping on anything.

Tina E. calls the crew over to meet us. They take their sweet, old time. Can't says I blame 'em. We likely wore out our welcome a few hours into Serpentine marathon. Now playing: "Sex Under the Blood Moon," from the *Sanguine Surf* Motion Picture Soundtrack.

A group of ten assembles in front of Tina and the boys. A mix of straight faces and forced smiles. Tina puts names to faces. They press flesh, in some cases reluctantly.

Jules (V.O.): It was a typical mix of archetypes and normal folk. I sized 'em up as they came and remembered the names of the ones that left some kind of impression. The rest were just background faces categorized by some distinguishable feature. There was...

- Dennings (Early 40s)... Too busy portraying himself as the hero-faced, Jim Brown-type that his appearance suggests to crack a smile. Either a decent guy or an insecure douchebag underneath it all. Gives me an overly firm handshake, but we'll let that slide.

- Mercer (30s)... Narrow-headed follower. Shifty-eyes. The Gilligan to Dennings' Skipper. Glances over at Dennings before shaking my hand.

- Kovach (40s)... Suburban dad with oddly jacked arms. Mildly effeminate. Gives the most genuine smile. Says he's a huge fan. Mental note: Potential alley should things go south here.

- Starr (aka) Motormouth (late 20s)... Thana's baby sister. Wasp-waisted ingénue who looks like she's seen too much. Detached. Eyes that look right through you. Seems older than her years. Maybe a little unhinged. Otherwise, extremely doable.

And the background players...

Scarface.
Five-head.
Short-arms.
Z'Dar.
Shar-Pei.
Fraidy-Cat.

Gramps attempts to break the ice with a self-deprecating remark about the marathon. Nobody laughs. Then Holly cuts in like he needs to get something off his chest.

"I'm sure it took a lot of resources to put all this together, let alone the juice to run it," he goes. "We appreciate the gesture, but do you really think it's a good idea to..."

Tina E. interrupts him all serious-like. "It's what Caleb wants."

Tina E. elects Dennings to show us around the venue. He begrudgingly accepts. Fuck you, too. Buddy. First words outta this guy's mouth once he gets us alone, "No offense, but if I never hear another one of your songs, it won't be soon enough."

"I hear ya, brother," Holly goes. "I think any of us would feel the same way in your shoes."

Dennings warms up to us from that point on.

"Thana would've loved it, though," he says with a smile.

He takes us to a pair of double doors in the back of the room marked Corridor C, and says, "Caleb wants to have her come in through these doors."

"Her?" I go. "Whaddaya got a dancer, too?"

Dennings makes a face like somebody farted. Then a DJ comes over the PA.

"Greetings, people of Earth," he goes like a rasped-voiced cartoon. "This is your friend in the sky. Your chaperone across the infected airwaves. Your brother from another mother; Mads Angle guiding you on a trip down memory lane with legendary rockers, Serpentine."

"Mads Angle, huh?" I go, trying to place the name and the voice.

"The used car salesman," Denning says.

Gramps gets all excited, "The one with the whacked-out commercials?! 'Mads is Mad, Mad, Mad about moving these cars!'"

"The one and only," Dennings says.

"I'm happy to report that the boys have arrived safely and are currently touring the facility in preparation for tomorrow's concert," Mads continues over the PA. "Next up for you Great Plains drifters is the group's 4th album, and my personal favorite "Ophidiophobia" to provide musical accompaniment as you make your way to the cafeteria for supper... er excuse me... dinner. Take it away boys."

Video (Great Plains CCTV Cam – Various / Canon Vixia HF HD Cam)

Cafeteria

A short line at the serving station. A portly man in an apron slings Ramen noodles with a long, handled soup-ladle. Serpentine marathon on the PA. The tables are empty save for a pair in the front of the room populated by two-dozen residents of the Great Plains Settlement. Familiar faces mixed with new background players talk amongst themselves and steal glances at the next table over where Jules, Graeme, and Hollister are seated side-by-side. The Vixia, mounted on a mini-tripod, at the far end of the boys' table.

Jules (V.O.): Ramen noodles and the usual conversation filtered through a most-popular-kids-in-high-school vibe, thanks to the cafeteria setting.

"Love your music; especially *this* song or *that* album." Ophidiophobia seems to be the favorite.

"How'd you guys meet?"

"Is the rockstar lifestyle really as crazy as it seems?"

"What's it like to have more money than God?"

"Is *this* rumor or *that* rumor true?"

"Heard you were friends with/dated (fill in random celebrity). What's he/she like?"

There were the usual jealous fucks trying too hard to act like they didn't give a rat's ass. I know everyone can't be a fan, but come on, guys. I counted three more doable chicks. Of course they were eyeing up Gramps. Pretty fucker. We all connected over our love of the Stone Show. A few of them lamented about how they'd rather be listening to the show than endure another second of the marathon. "No offense. I love you guys, but Jesus H. Christ," one goes. That seemed to be a common theme.

Video (Canon Vixia HF HD Cam)

Room 262

A large, windowless storage room made to resemble a hotel suite. Framed photos of Maryland landmarks hang from the walls. Three folding cots draped in sheets and plush comforters. A fluffy pillow at the head of each. A mint resting on top. An end-table/dresser set. The Vixia atop the dresser, mounted on the mini-tripod. A quaint, bedside lamp on the end-table. A TV/DVD combo on the dresser. A stack of DVDs beside it. A thin, rectangular mirror mounted on the back of the door.

The boys in mid-discussion. Graeme is laid out on his back on one of the cots while Jules and Hollister walk around casually inspecting the room as they talk. Their cots claimed by a backpack resting on top of each one.

Jules (V.O.): Caleb set us up in an old storage room far from the other residents. Said he wanted to give us space to ourselves to prepare mentally for the show. A stack of our favorite movies on the dresser; shit only a real fan would know. Impressive. We made a sweep for bugs and hidden cams, then gossiped about the residents. Gramps called dibs on Motormouth and Tina E.—assuming she and Caleb aren't already a couple. Kinda got that sense from their interaction.

"Tina E?!" I go. "Maybe if you want your cock bitten off."

Gramps makes the case that the crazy/intense ones are usually the best in bed. "And it ain't like we'll see each other again after tomorrow," he goes. Couldn't argue with him on that. Besides, that left the other three doable chicks for me and Holly to choose from. We get a passive aggressive scolding from Holly, who thinks we're being seduced by our surroundings.

"This place is okay, and all," I go. "But it ain't the Grotto."

Holly gives me this *don't bullshit me* look, and says. "You know what I mean."

He was talking about all the adulation from Caleb Kaiser, the concert set-up, that mindfuck of a video-teaser on the planetarium screen, and the dinner-time idol-worship. It had been awhile since we'd experienced anything on this level. And the fact that all of it tied into some false sense of security we might be feeling from the Weather invite and how that's liable to make us careless, if we lose sight of it.

I get all pissed and go, "Wait-a-minute... Weren't you the one who was all Gung Ho about coming here in the first place?"

We're interrupted by a knock at the door. We all freeze for no real reason other than the fact that it caught us off guard in the middle of a slightly heated moment. Caleb's voice comes through the door shortly after.

"Sorry to disturb you, guys. It's Caleb."

Me and Holly look at each other, thinking the same thing, "Did he hear that last exchange?"

Hollister walks over and opens the door to reveal Caleb Kaiser standing with a short, broad, chocolate-skinned man (Dr. Chacha Mokae, 60s). Tina Escalante's pinched face floating between them.

Caleb makes a face like he was working out some odd, drug-induced kink and then goes, "Hope I'm not interrupting anything."

Me and Gramps respond at the same time, "No," and sound guilty as fuck.

He introduces Doc Mokae, who comes off as humorless and full of wisdom. He forces a smile and corrects Caleb's mispronunciation of his name in an accent out of Africa.

"Cha cha. Like the dance?" I go, smiling in case he didn't get the joke. He seemed like the type who wouldn't.

He dismisses me with a look. Like I said. Humorless.

Video (Great Plains CCTV Cam – Various / Canon Vixia HD Cam – Graeme's POV)

Concrete Corridors

Caleb Kaiser and Chacha Mokae lead the boys to the control room. Tina Escalante at the rear.

Jules (V.O.): Doc Mokae's got a voice made for long speeches, and a weird, almost hypnotic cadence that deserved a crunchy blues/rock guitar lick playing underneath it. I couldn't help fingerin' strings in my head while he spoke. I ask him right away about Dr. Hammond and what went down at their settlement in Downingtown. He says that he left before all that. Something about differences of opinion. Hmmm. He was eager to change the subject, but my curious ass kept changing it back until Holly scolds me with his usual, "Jules!"

Gramps tosses out a joke that pretty much sums up what we're all thinking.

"This place sure ain't short on hallways," he goes.

"Control room's not much further," Caleb says. Apparently he's got something important to show us.

Caleb is a bit more reserved this time, almost like someone had given him a stern talking-to between our initial meeting and now.

Doc Mokae starts going on about the Devil-in-the-details...

Doc Mokae: Whoever coined that phrase couldn't have been more correct. It's in the little nuisances. That's where the real answers hide. Take the common cold, for example. The virus might manifest in one person as sore-throat, body aches, while another experiences a mild cough, congestion, runny nose, and yet another, experiences a mild sense of lethargy and discomfort. What I'm saying is that this virus is no different?

Caleb: We've all seen it. The deadheads that linger in the background, uninterested in the feeding frenzy going on a few feet away, seemingly obsessed with carrying out some vague memory of a mundane task during life.

Graeme: Like at all the supermarkets and banks.

Doc Mokae: Exactly... And airports, and hospitals, and shopping malls. All these places where people gathered. We see, in these subjects, traces of their former selves carrying on through the fog of infection. It's not many. But you see them in every town you pass through. The virus has turned them. Yes. But not enough to completely subjugate who they were as a person. Or enough to make them crave human flesh. I've even seen subjects who were actually repulsed by the act.

Me and Holly converse via glances while Gramps breaks into some anecdotes that we've either heard a million times or seen with our own eyes.

-The deadfuck in the SUV that kept ramming it into the wall with the mural of a road on it.
-The deadfuck flasher.

At some point Holly goes, "I'm assuming there's a point to all this."

Control Room

A small room. A bank of live monitors cover two of the four walls. A curved, multi-buttoned console stretches the length of the monitor collage. A slight, bald man in a beat-up Gabardine Rockabilly Jacket that had clearly belonged to someone else (Mads Angle - Late 60s) operates the console from a swiveling office chair. An oversized joint pinched between his fingertips. The images onscreen map out the park and the subterranean utilidor system in grainy video and through a pungent veil of marijuana smoke. The front gate. The amusement park. Stairwells and hallways. Cafeteria. Storage rooms. Planetarium.

Mads Angle whips around as Caleb enters and fans away the pungent veil...

Caleb (to Mads): Don't you ever get enough of that crap?

Caleb waits for everyone to enter. Tina elects to wait outside.

She closes the door behind them. Mads Angle's eyes light up with genuine enthusiasm when he sees the boys.

Mads: Hail-motherfucking-Serpentine! In-the-flesh!"

He leans back and drinks the boys in as if to validate their existence.

Mads: You know, "Ride the Serpentine" was the soundtrack to many a conquests in my younger days. But I'm sure you hear that all the time.

Jules (V.O.): I couldn't help but smile when I saw Mads Angle, even though he looked like a stoned, squinty-eyed, shriveled husk instead of the jolly, round loud-mouth I remember from his commercials.

Jules: Not lately.

He takes a big whiff.

Jules: Smells like good shit.

Graeme: I was gonna say the same thing.

Mads: The best.

Mads eyes the fattie like it held the answers to the meaning of life… and you could fuck it.

Mads: Didn't think you boys would actually come.

He leans forward and offers Jules a toke. He accepts.

Jules: Don't mind if I do.

Mads finger-rolls the joint to Jules, who takes a long toke, and holds it in. He makes a satisfied expression as he blows out a vertical plume of smoke.

Jules (V.O): It'd been a *loong* time since I had shit this good.

I could tell right away from the taste.

Jules hands the joint to the right and get no takers. Graeme is standing next to him, white as a ghost, again. A combination of utter confusion and terror shapes his expression. His eyes are fixed on the monitor bank. His arms hang by his sides, the Vixia in his right hand, the "Record" button still lit. Hollister is standing on the other side of Graeme, equally shaken.

Jules' head whips between the monitor-bank and his bandmates, trying to ascertain the cause of their sudden alarm. Too many images to choose from.

Graeme backs away pointing at a Monitor 26.

Monitor 26

A room-sized walk-in freezer. Cold. Windowless. Insulated steel walls peeking out from behind a collage of posters and photos neatly cut from magazines. Graeme Gunz featured prominently in each poster/photo--a mixture of candid and professionally-posed shots. A woman stands with her back to the camera facing the rear wall. Ace bandage wrapped around little more than bone from the neck down and decorated with random stains of varying sizes and degrees of darkness. Ripped jeans and a Ride the Serpentine Concert Tee hang slack from her near-skeletal frame. Legs like double-wrapped toothpicks shake under her weight. She labors to hold her right arm extended toward the photo directly in front of her—Graeme frozen in mid-song, shirtless and glistening with sweat. Sultry, beckoning eyes peek out from behind a cascade of hair.

The woman is motionless, seemingly transfixed.

Control Room

Jules (V.O.): My first thought, after picking my jaw up off the floor, was that Thana Kaiser was up to her old tricks, and what I was looking at was just some poor deadfuck that she had projected onto. Then it settled in just how... different she looked. If Mads Angle was a shell of his former self, than Thana was a low-light shadow. Gramps steals the moment.

Graeme: Is this... Is she?

Mads: Live and in stereo from the old freezer in the B wing.

Hollister's alarm turns to suspicion.

Caleb: I know how it seems. Keeping her like this for so long. But, I assure you that my motives are...

Graeme: No. It's not that. It's...

Jules (scolding): Gramps!

Jules gestures, "No," to an exasperated Graeme.

Jules (V.O.): I thought it better to hear Caleb out before we go jumping to epic conclusions that could jeopardize our credibility with these people. Believe me, I was halfway there, myself.

Caleb: They found her wandering half-a-mile from the crash site. I had to see her again. To say goodbye. I wanted to be the one to end her suffering. So, I had them bring her back here. But then something happened...

Caleb stops speaking to work through his emotions.

Mads clears his throat and the boys nearly jump out of their skins. He extends an arm toward Jules.

Mads (re: joint): You done with that?

Jules can't get rid of the thing fast enough.

Caleb gathers himself and nods at Doc Mokae, who then grabs a walkie-talkie clipped to his belt and speaks into it.

Doc Mokae (into walkie-talkie): Okay, Lance.

Monitor 26

An unarmed man (Lance, 30s) nervously enters the room. We recognize him as one of the forgettable faces from the cafeteria. Lance tosses a worried expression at the CCTV Camera and then moves toward Living Dead Thana. He clears his throat to get her attention.

Thana turns slowly. Her face is a decayed memory, all sunken in with highlights of exposed bone. A mask of frost stiffens her expression and emphasizes the blue tones in her leathery skin. Lazy eyes floating beneath desiccated corneas eventually come upon the man. She cricks her head to the side as if trying to recall his identity, yet it all remains on the tip of her infected, undead tongue.

Control Room

Caleb (to Mads): Kill the music.

Mads flips a switch and the music stops playing. Cheers from the planetarium on Monitor 4.

Monitor 26

Thana's rigid expression shifts from vague curiosity to hunger. Her dead eyes swell with wanting. A predatory frown manipulates what's left of her features. A snarl pushes through horribly cracked lips.

Lance backs away as Undead Thana lumbers toward him, gaining enthusiasm with each wobbly step. She reaches for him as best she can under the strain of depleted muscle, fingers grasping the shrinking space between them. Lance looks up at the camera.

Lance (nervous): Any day now guys…

A few seconds pass…

Lance (panicked): GUYS!

The music returns and instantly lulls Thana back into a semi-serene state. She seems confused as to how she ended up in Lance's personal space as he stands there with his back pressed against the wall, his face turned away from her. Eyes squeezed shut. He opens one eye, and exhales in relief before slinking out from in front of her. He turns angrily toward the camera.

Lance (angry): *That was WAY too close, man! WAY too close!*

He storms from the room and slams the door shut behind him.

Control Room

Mads (to Caleb): That *was* pretty close.

Caleb ignores the comment and turns to the boys, all three of them experiencing some degree of shock.

Caleb (re: Thana): You see... She's still in there... Thanks to the doctor's implant.

Graeme: Implant?

Caleb: A microchip.

Doc Mokae: Three of them, to be exact. An extension of Dr. Hammond's research.

Caleb: Maybe it's only a small part of my Thana left, but as long as there's even a glimmer, I have to try and reach her. For the sake of what we had. She would do the same for me. I have to try... With the doctor's help. With *YOUR* help.

The music scores an awkward moment as the boys look to each other for a response.

95

Caleb: I'm talking about the concert, of course. That's why I stressed that the setlist be the same as the one in '87, and that the planetarium look as close to that night as possible. It's where Thana was going when she died... Where she thought she was going...

Doc Mokae: It was a significant moment in her life. By recreating it, we might be able to bring her around fully... if only for a short time.

Hollister: For a short time?!

Doc Mokae: It doesn't always work, especially with a subject in such an advance stage of...

He glances at Caleb and edits his thought on the fly.

Doc Mokae: Nevertheless, I believe it can still be accomplished.

Caleb: At the rate these vaccine trucks are being raided, we're gonna need more options for dealing with this thing. And quick.

Hollister: How do the other residents here feel about...?

Caleb (interrupts): The last thing I said to my wife before she ran off that night was that I wish she had died instead of our son Willem. She was completely lost to the delusion by that point. I was so frustrated. I just wanted my Thana back. Do you have any idea how that feels? I have to make it right. In spite of what everyone thinks. I have to... And if it helps the doctor to find a cure or some method of treating this infection, then all the better. Already, we've seen signs that the increased brain activity from the multiple implants slows decomposition. Tell 'em, Doc. Go on. Tell 'em.

Doc Mokae: To some degree. Yes.

The boys work to digest the news while an eager Caleb awaits their reactions. The marathon rolls on through the PA. Undead Thana on TV. Doc Mokae analyzing her performance like a stage-parent. Mads Angle leaning way back in his swivel-chair like a stoned couch-potato.

A minute later…

Jules is struck by a sudden thought.

Jules (to Doc Mokae): What you're doing here… It wouldn't have anything to do with the… *disagreement* between you and Dr. Hammond. Would it? I mean… I imagine it'd be pretty terrifying to wake up and see yourself that way, only to find out that you've got just a short time until you go back to it.

The remark momentarily disrupts the doctor's clinical demeanor. Annoyed, he appears to mull over the appropriate retort. It takes a while…

Mads Angle breaks the ice.

Mads: Now. That, right there, is what we call 'suspense,' folks.

Doc Mokae (to Jules): You are correct in your assessment. My colleagues and I did not exactly see eye-to-eye on the ethics of such research. They felt that we were skirting the ethical line as it was. Dr. Hammond's intention was simply to gain control of the subject on a rudimentary level. Just enough to control basic motor functions, for example. My intention is to reach the essence of the subject, the person they were before the infection took hold. My implants target the frontal, occipital, and the temporal lobes. These are the areas associated with personality, attention, decision-making, perception, memory, recognition…

Video (Canon Vixia HF HD Cam)

Room 262

The Vixia perched atop the dresser. Jules and Hollister are

97

seated close together on one of the cots while an incredulous Graeme paces in the background.

Jules (V.O.): Graeme was busy thinking himself in circles as he tried to make sense of things. Holly was finally onboard the "This was a bad idea," train and looking to rendezvous with the "Let's get the fuck outta here," express. Funny how the tables turn. After racking my brain, I had finally settled on, "It is what it is." At this point I wouldn't be surprised if Santa Claus was real.

Holly wanted to run tonight, at lights out. Just like the Grotto. But I thought it better to go with the flow than try to escape from a place we weren't familiar with.

Hollister: They'll never be the wiser.

Jules: We had months to get to know the Grotto, man. We don't know this place like that.

Hollister: I plan on getting to know it tonight.

Jules (V.O.): Caleb had assigned Dennings to escort Holly out to the back lot after dark to search for a battery.

Hollister: We're all set once we find a battery.

Jules looks to Graeme for support, but he's still pacing and mumbling about spooks and ESP.

Graeme: Supposedly the psychic center is located in the right hemisphere of the brain. Maybe the doc's implant somehow…

Jules (interrupts): How, the fuck, do you even know that? Huh? All you're gonna come away with from all that *supposing* is a massive-fucking-headache. Trust me. It is what it is, man. Say it with me.

Graeme rolls his eyes and continues to pace and mumble.

Jules (to Hollister): Look. Caleb seems like an alright dude, but he's clearly damaged. And you know what? I don't fucking blame him. But, in his mind, we are the key to bringing Thana around. Don't you think he's gonna feel some kinda way about us leavin', let alone sneakin' out under his nose. We've dealt with enough crazy fucks to know how badly that could go.

Hollister: But what's gonna happen when she doesn't come around? The doc's got Caleb drinking the Kool Aid, big time. And did you see the way he kept looking to Tina E for approval? What's that all about?

Jules (V.O.): I had thought the same thing. You couldn't deny that there was a whiff of something living in Thana Kaiser. The fact that it took our music to bring it to the surface was, at the same time, strangely gratifying and creepy as fuck. But Caleb was delusional to think that she would ever be close to the woman he remembered. And even if Doc Mokae did manage to bring her back, I would think watching your dead/alive wife come apart mentally once she realizes what happened to her, what she is, and what's going to happen to her again, would be worse than the first time she died. But like I said, I don't blame him.

Jules: We're on the same page, brother. I just think we should wait, at least until after the concert. That way we've got tonight and tomorrow to get to know this place, in case we need to book on the sneak. I don't even think it's gonna come to that, to be honest. Caleb's gonna see what he wants to see. And I'm guessing his people are gonna go right along with it. Bing. Bang. Boom. And we're on our way to the Weather.

As Hollister contemplates, Graeme walks up and thrusts a torn sheet of paper in his and Jules' faces. On one side, a note written in lipstick, and signed with a heart. A crudely sketched map on the other.

Graeme (whispers, re: note): Somebody slid it under the door.

99

Jules: Just now?!

Graeme immediately shushes him. They continue the conversation in whisper-tones.

Graeme: Had to be since we got back from the control room. It wasn't there when we first came in.

Jules: You sure? Maybe we missed it in all the excitement.

Hollister: It wasn't there. I would've seen.

Jules takes the note. Looks it over.

Note: "To Graeme Gunz - 7pm. Southeast doors. Something important to show you."

Jules (to Graeme): Surprise. Surprise. You gonna do it?

Graeme: I don't know, man. To be completely honest, I'm so creeped-the-fuck-out over Thana that I ain't even thinking like that.

Jules: Well... If you don't, I will. I could use the stress relief.

Graeme snatches the note from Jules, thinks it over. He walks over and checks his appearance in the mirror.

Hollister (to Graeme): You gonna film it?

Graeme gives him a look, *"Ewwwww."*

Hollister: Whoever it is might really have something important to show you.

Jules: Other than her cooch?

Graeme finishes primping and fishes a leather case from his backpack. A variety of spy cameras inside. He grabs a pair of designer spy-glasses and slides them on his face. He fixes his hair into a ponytail.

100

Jules (to Graeme, re: glasses): Where'd Gramps go? Who are you?

Graeme makes a face. "Fuck off!"

Jules: Just trying to lighten the mood.

Graeme (re: glasses): Don't get your hopes up, ya pervy fucks. Anything happens and I'm taking 'em off.

Video (Spy-glasses Cam - Graeme's POV)

South Corridor

A darker section of the utilidor system. Graeme standing in a recessed doorway, inspecting his surroundings. Steel double-doors marked MAIN PARK SOUTH to his rear. A long hallway in front of him. Concrete walls and blue pipes. CCTV Cameras. A darkened intersection 50ft away. SOUTH CORRIDOR stenciled on the wall.

Graeme (V.O.): Wishful thinking kept me stuck on Tina E. and Motormouth. I hadn't realized how long it'd been since I've had some strange until I was standing there going down the list of pros and cons for each one. Tina E had the intensity. Motormouth had that quiet sex appeal. I played both scenarios out in my head. By the end of it my dick was so hard it fucking hurt. I'm literally looking down at my dong, begging the fucker to ease back, when I hear footsteps.

A man appears at the mouth of the intersection. He is shrouded in darkness from the waist, up. We don't see him until he's already walking toward us.

Graeme (V.O.): I look up and see one of the guys from the planetarium coming down the hall. The one who looks like a jacked Lifetime Channel husband. Kovach is his name. He looks worried, antsy. Like a guy expecting to get caught. So, I'm fumbling with my dick, which is like a fucking diving board by now. I'm trying to tuck it up under my belt as this guy walks up on me and says...

Kovach: Who else knows about this?

Graeme (V.O.): I'm too busy looking over his shoulder for something with a vagina to appear.

Kovach: You didn't tell Caleb. Did you?

Graeme: No. Just the guys.

Kovach: The guys?

Graeme: Jules and Holly.

Graeme (V.O.): Ya dumbass. Who, the fuck, else would I be talking about?

Kovach: Oh.

Kovach exhales like he just found out the baby wasn't his. His expression and posture relax. He smiles warmly, offers his hand.

Kovach: I'm Doug Kovach. Most people just call me Kovach. Never thought I looked much like a Doug. Feel like I haven't had a chance to properly introduce myself… with everything going on around here.

Graeme is still glancing over his shoulder as they shake hands.

Graeme: Soooo, it's just you?

Kovach: You disappointed?

Graeme (V.O.): I wanted to say, "Hell-fucking-yes, I'm disappointed," but what fell outta my mouth instead was a knee-jerk response.

Graeme: Of course not!

Graeme (V.O.): Seemed like the dude was getting off on my discomfort.

Kovach: I'm loving the glasses, by the way.

Graeme: So, what's this big secret?

He looks around like he's expecting to catch a pair of eyes peeking out from behind a wall, and then gestures toward the doors.

Kovach: This way.

Main Park South

Kovach leads Graeme on a pre-determined route through the amusement park at night. Hulking shadows looming from the sidelines. A captive audience of floating eyes and disembodied smiles gone demonic under the creepy, crawly spell of darkness. Sleeping giants of steel and wood in the middle distance. CCTV cameras. Megaphones pumping out dead wailing.

Graeme (V.O.): He takes me down this path like the one we walked in on. You think this place is creep-city in the daytime... Image that times 10. You know how I have that—used to have—that irrational fear of seeing life-like statues at the bottom of the ocean? That's what it reminded me off out there. He tells me that they got Mads to turn off the cameras out here and in the South Corridor. "He's on our side," he says.

Graeme (to Kovach): Where the hell're we going?

Kovach: Shhhh! (whispers) Someplace we can talk.

A 75-foot replica of the statue of liberty's arm, from the forearm to the torch, sticking out of the ground. A door in the meat of the forearm. Graeme follows Kovach up to the door and inside.

Statue

Kovach leads Graeme up a rickety spiral staircase and out onto a narrow observation deck surrounding the base of the torch-flame. Graeme whimpers in disapproval at the see-through, lattice-work flooring. He hesitates before following Kovach out onto the deck.

Kovach gestures for Graeme to stay low as he works his way up to the edge of the deck, sits down, and dangles his legs over the edge. The railing is his armrest. He has done this before. A nervous Graeme reluctantly follows.

The observation deck looks out onto a blackened cityscape. Familiar structures silhouetted against the deep blue tones in the lower sky. A vast parking lot on the park's rear border stocked with a variety of abandoned and found vehicles. A steady crowd of undead pressed against the border fence. Rather than labor to push through, they stagger, and sway, and tremble, and stand there sedate, collectively transfixed by the dead medley coming from the megaphones. In the dark they appear as a singular, multi-headed, multi-limbed, pulsating entity.

Graeme (V.O.): It was like looking down on some whacked out city floating in space. That's how dark it was. You know how I am about heights, so it was actually better that I could hardly see a thing up there. In the dark, the deadfucks looked like cockroaches moving under a sheet.

Kovach leans back onto his hands and lets his legs swing. He smiles at the blackened cityscape.

Kovach: From up here it's almost peaceful.

Graeme is seated upright, anxious. He stares straight ahead holding the railing in a white-knuckled death-grip. He stiffens when the breeze kicks up out of fear that it might blow him off of the deck.

Graeme (sarcastic): Yeah. Peaceful. That's exactly what I was thinking.

Kovach points to a pile of cigarette butts nearby.

Kovach: This is a popular spot. I used to come here with my... with Steve before he died.

Graeme: Why'd you bring me here?

Graeme (V.O.): The dude starts telling me all this shit about Caleb Kaiser. How he was this great leader, but he's been in no shape to run things since Thana died. How Tina E's been keeping him real close since then. How she's got him all drugged up.

Kovach: That bit about us being nearly out of ammo... Not true. Well... as far as Caleb and the Escalantes know it is. A decision was made to hide the weapons and ammo when Tina and her brothers started making trouble. The fire in the weapons shack was deliberately set as a cover. No one here trusts them. Not from the first time Dennings and Mercer brought them here. They found them during a supply run a few months in. Tina cozies up to Caleb, right off the bat. She gets him to appoint her brothers in key positons with security. Now they're essentially running things.

Caleb and Tina developed a *thing* on the side while Thana was still alive. It got pretty hot-and-heavy and Caleb even talked about leaving his wife for her. But that all changed when his son Willem died and Thana started to slip. Then, when *she* died, it broke him. He latched onto Tina as a means of support. And she took advantage of his weakened state.

She claims that her entire family was in the Colombian Military. She was in the medical corps and her no-neck brothers were infantry. Because of her medical background, she acts like she knows what's best for Caleb. One thing's for damn sure. (leans closer) That bitch knows her way around a pharmacy.

She's as obsessed with Caleb as *he* is with bringing Thana back to life. She can't stand that he still pines for her. That's why it didn't make sense when she came up with the idea to have the concert. But everybody was into it, at first... even though we suspected that she had ulterior motives. We figured, at the very least, that it would help Caleb gain some closure. Maybe snap him out of his shell-shock. This was before we knew that he and Doc Mokae had gone out, and found Thana, and that they were keeping her here as some kinda guinea pig. We only just found out about that.

Graeme: He was keeping it from everyone? Shit... I didn't know that. That's so... 80s horror. If you know what I mean. Not to belittle your situation... Just forget I even said that.

Kovach: It's cool. Just the fact that I'm actually sitting here with you... As a fan... It's a nice break from the tension around here lately.

Graeme: I got a sense that something was up during dinner.

Kovach: It's gotten really bad since we found that they were keeping Thana here. Especially for her sister Starr. Thana may have been flakey as all get-out, but she would never want to walk around like that. Everyone knows that. Caleb knows it, too. But he's blinded by this idea that he can bring her back. Tina won't let anyone near him, to try and talk some sense into him. She claims he's too emotionally drained to deal with all our drama. Can you believe that?

Graeme: It hit us pretty hard, too.

Kovach looks confused. Graeme attempts to clarify as if maybe he's said too much.

Graeme: You know... Just the thought of it... Keeping your dead wife locked in a freezer.

For a while they sit in silent appreciation of the landscape below. Kovach stealing glances on the sly.

Kovach: I'm not supposed to tell you this next part. They're afraid you guys will run.

106

Graeme is suddenly concerned.

Graeme: Tell me what? Who's afraid?

Kovach: Dennings and the others.

Graeme: Tell me what?

Kovach hesitates.

Kovach: The concert was just a front to get you guys here. Tina means to use you to collect some kind of ransom from the government. She has no intention of letting you leave.

Graeme shudders. His grip on the railing tightens. He turns to Kovach. His voice climbs several octaves.

Graeme: What?! You're serious?!

Kovach nods.

Kovach: As a heart attack. It's supposed to go down sometime after the concert. Mercer overheard Tina and one of her brothers going over their plan. We're pretty sure she's keeping Caleb in the dark about it. He'd never be a party to that shit. And who knows what she'll do if he doesn't go along with it. Tina is definitely an "If I can't have him, nobody can," type-of-bitch, if you know what I mean.

Graeme is incredulous. Kovach watches with guilty eyes.

Kovach: The rest of us are prepared to do whatever it takes to make sure that doesn't happen. Just so you know.

Graeme (unconvinced): And how, exactly, do you plan to do that?

Kovach: We have a plan. Footage from the CCTV cameras of the shit the Escalantes have been up to. I was going to show you some of it tonight, but Mads didn't have it ready in time. Fucking stoner. We're gonna play the footage on the big screen during the concert. This way Caleb will see those *sorry-asses* for what they really are. Then we give the Escalantes two options. Leave. Or be killed. They won't expect us to be armed. But we will be.

Graeme thinks for a moment.

Graeme: You don't think Caleb will have a problem with you threatening to kill Tina?

Kovach: Not after what we show him. Don't worry. We've got it all worked out. We're even willing to arm each of you, if it'll make you feel better.

Graeme: Why not just take the place back, if you got them outnumbered and outgunned?

Kovach: And risk losing Caleb to that bitch? Or risk that she might hurt him in some way? You don't understand. She's got him zonked out worse than those flesh-eaters out there. Except when she wants him to perform. Like when they walked you guys through earlier. We were watching from the CCTV cameras.

Graeme: So... In a way, you and your people are using us, too.

Kovach: We had no choice. The concert will be the first time we've had access to Caleb in weeks.

Graeme doesn't respond.

Kovach: We would all be dead if it wasn't for that man. And I don't just mean from outside influences. We were coming apart as a group in the beginning. No one could agree on anything or even get along. Always scheming. Always fighting. It got to the point where nobody knew who to trust. Caleb Kaiser... he managed to pull us together. To help us to look past our differences and relate to each other on a human level. Without him, I don't think we would've survived.

Kovach is distracted by something in the darkness below. He leans forward and points toward the parking lot.

Kovach: There they are; Dennings and Hollister.

A pair of fidgety beams of light dance between rows of vehicles in the rear lot.

Kovach: Dennings will have you guys fixed-up in no time.

Graeme: Based on what you just told me, "No time" ain't soon enough.

Kovach: We're good people here, Graeme. I promise you. But we've had to learn the hard way that if we're going to survive this, we have to adapt. I really am sorry it has to go down like this.

Graeme stares straight ahead, deep in thought. Kovach appears fascinated by Graeme's inner turmoil. Some time passes.

Kovach: We put our idols up on such pedestals... It's kinda nice to see that you're human... er... vulnerable, just like the rest of us.

Kovach lays his hand on top of Graeme's.

Kovach: It makes you even more attractive, in my opinion.

Graeme turns toward Kovach…

Graeme: Are you kidding me…

…and is met by Kovach moving in for a kiss. Graeme turns away at the last second and puts his arm between them. He shoves Kovach to arm's length just as his lips make contact with Graeme's left cheek, his other hand clutching the railing for dear life… and leverage.

Graeme: Whoa! What the fuck, dude?!

Kovach overreacts to the rise in Graeme's voice.

Kovach: Shhhhhhh! Quiet! They'll hear you!

Graeme's posture deflates. Kovach's consternation morphs into embarrassment.

Kovach: I'm sorry. I'm sorry. Oh Gawdddd...

Graeme: It's okay.

Kovach: I'm *sooo* sorry. I just thought... You know. Because of that rumor...

Graeme: Yeah. Well. Don't believe everything you read in the tabloids.

Kovach slaps his hands over his face and wears them like a mask.

Kovach (into hands): I feel so stupid.

Graeme: Don't sweat it, man. No hard feelings.

Kovach lets out an exasperated grunt. He lowers his hands and stares blankly into the darkness. Graeme watches the fidgety beams of light as a distraction from the uncomfortable silence.

Kovach: It says a lot about you that didn't go all apeshit like a lotta straight guys would've. Thanks for that. Makes me like you even more, unfortunately.

Graeme turns to face Kovach, who throws his hands up in jest.

Kovach: Don't worry. I'm not gonna try anything else.

Graeme chuckles.

Graeme: When you've lived the kinda lifestyle we did for

so long, any prejudices you might've had growing up are completely wiped away.

Kovach nods, taking it in.

Graeme: Even if the rumor was true... What, the fuck gave you the impression that this was a good time to go in for a kiss?

Kovach thinks for a moment. A smile takes shape.

Kovach: Desperate times call for desperate measures, I guess.

Video (Canon Vixia HF HD Cam)

Room 262

Montage. The boys seated close together, deep in discussion, walking around, lying awake on their cots, stretching, exercising. The Vixia perched atop the dresser.

Jules (V.O.): We stayed up all night trying to pull a Plan B out our asses in case Kovach and the Great Plains Posse's plan went south. Gramps was all about diversions; first by setting a fire, like they had done with the weapons shack. Then by somehow letting in the deadfucks. Holly wanted to take it right to the Escalantes. Fuck waiting 'til after the concert. He's all, "We'll pop 'em from the stage if we have to."

I was busy tossing out commentary on the pros and cons—mostly the cons—of each of their ideas and sniping on about how we'd be living like kings at the Weather and rocking out on the Martin Stone Show if Holly would've listened to me from the start. I could see that he was getting tired of hearing about it.

We take a short break from the discussion to lament about Stone Show withdrawal.

We ultimately decided to play it by ear. If things started to look wonky—or hinky, as Holly would say—then we'd go with his plan and take them out from the stage. Chances are all three of us are better shots than anyone here. Don't ask me how I know that. It's just a feeling.

By morning we were like manic bobble-heads fading in and out of sleep.

"Ok. Boys!" Holly claps and sends me and Gramps into a momentary panic. "No more fucking around. If we're gonna do this, then let's *DO THIS!*"

We spend the next half-an-hour doing the saddest calisthenics routine you ever saw. Holly, our de facto drill sergeant/motivational speaker, offers up gems like, "Buck up, campers. It's not like we've never played a gig under duress before."

"This ain't exactly the usual pre-show jitters we're dealing with here," I go.

"No gig's too small," he says, trying to throw back some of the shit I've been giving him.

"At least we'll be armed," Graeme says.

"So they say," I go. "I'll feel a whole helluva-lot-better when I've actually got a weapon in my hand."

Video (Great Plains CCTV Cam – Various / Canon Vixia HF HD Cam)

Planetarium

A stage aglow in rhythmic spotlights. On its surface, the members of Serpentine sling magic in the form of warm-up licks, and riffs, and drum-beat haiku beneath a kinetic sky made of images, videos, concert footage, and movie clips from their past. The Vixia mounted on a tripod near the drums.

An uneasy crowd is spread throughout the second and third rows that surround the stage. Twenty faces hiding secrets. They appear restless. Preoccupied. Their focus is split between the stage and a pair of doors marked CORRIDOR C.

Rings of empty chairs ripple away from the stage and into the dark background. Bursts of colorful light from the image-storm above assails the dark majority. A hulking insectoid shape becomes a planetarium projector. Two upright forms become Christian and Mateo Escalante; one posted on each side of the Corridor C doors.

At some point, one of the brothers lifts his hand to his ear and then gestures toward the stage. Graeme acknowledges with a wave. He turns to his bandmates and nods.

Graeme: Here we go! Ah one! Ah two! Ah one! Two! THREE! FOUR!

Warm up licks build into something more substantial. Chords to a familiar anthem ride atop an agitated bassline. Drums become like rolling thunder. The overhead montage ends on old footage from the Baltimore Concert in '87.

Christian Escalante opens the door to a deafening chorus of cheers from the Baltimore fans on the screen. The Great Plains crowd is more interested in the multiple figures darkening the doorway to Corridor C.

Caleb Kaiser escorts Thana through the doorway. Her ripped jeans and concert tee have been laundered and sewed. They hang loose from her stick limbs. The wrapped under layer has been replaced with new bandage. A pillowcase covers her head. Her stiff, afflicted gait is further restricted by a dog-catcher pole tightened around her neck. At the other end of the pole, Tina Escalante guides Thana from behind with both hands. Doc Mokae follows them into the room.

Caleb scans the room and responds to the swell of curiosity directed his way with a look of contentment.

Graeme lifts the microphone to his mouth.

Graeme: Hello Baltimore! Are you ready to *ROCK*?!

The locals are hesitant. On the screen, the Baltimore '87 crowd reacts in unison. "YEAH!"

Graeme cups his hand to his ear and turns it to the local crowd.

Graeme: I SAID... *ARE YOU READY TO ROCK*?!

A few mouths move. A few faces broadcast fake excitement while side-eying the awkward procession down the aisle. Doc Mokae stays back, preferring to watch from the dark background.

On the screen, the Baltimore '87 crowd responds with even more enthusiasm. "YEEEAAAH!"

The extended opening salvo of agitated strings and rolling thunder gestates into a song called "Sinful Serenade." Graeme sways to the seductive chords. He closes his eyes and begins to sing.

Down in front, Tina escorts Thana to her seat. Front row. Center stage. She uses the catcher pole to hold her still while Caleb gently guides her into the seat next to him. Thana flinches in response to his touch. She turns her head away from the stage and faces him as if she can see through the pillowcase.

Caleb sits down next to his wife. Afterward he nods at Tina, who returns an unwilling glare. Caleb makes a face at her, "Do it! Now!"

Tina hesitates before releasing the wire loop around Thana's neck and sliding it over her head. Caleb sidles closer to her, her face still pointed at him. He slowly releases his hold on her, ready for a sudden burst of movement that never comes.

Tina backs out off into the aisle and stands there holding the dog-catcher pole vertically, like a passenger on a city bus.

Thana eventually turns back to the source of the familiar music. Caleb whispers something in her ear and then removes the pillowcase.

Thana's face is a ghastly sight teetering atop a narrow column of clean bandage. Patches of ashen skin stretched over visible bone. Her eyes are like shriveled orbs shoved into recessed pits. Her scalp is visible through dried wisps of thinned-out hair.

Horrified reactions from the peanut gallery. Motormouth in hysterics. Kovach consoles/restrains her.

Thana whips her head toward Caleb as fast as her rotten neck muscles will allow. Caleb cups her face in his hands and looks lovingly into her eyes. His touch tears away a patch of skin around her cheekbone, leaving it to dangle from her face. He shudders at his mistake, dismayed by the thought that he may have hurt her in any way. He works to reattach the dangling flap, gently poking and applying slight pressure to help it stick.

Thana turns back to the stage without warning. Her sudden movement tugs at the skin-flap, tearing it from her face completely. Caleb makes a hissing sound in sympathetic reaction. He looks down at the rigid, desiccated flap of skin pinched between his index finger and thumb. He half-attempts to replace it before changing his mind and carefully sliding it into the pocket of his sensible blazer.

Thana fixates on the long, lean serpent with the flowing mane writhing on the stage to an extended guitar solo. Indifference gives way to dumbfounded awe that seems beyond her living-dead capabilities. Everyone else watching her. Her head falls to an inquisitive lean or maybe it's just the result of waning neck support.

Graeme is in full serpent-mode. Eyes squeezed shut. His

115

face twisted in orgasmic delight. Jules and Hollister play on, attempting to stifle their growing concern. An oblivious Graeme continues to dance as Thana grasps the armrests of her chair and uses them to facilitate a frail ascension. Her arms, barely thicker than broomsticks, tremble under the stress, yet her eyes never leave the writhing serpent. Tina motions forward, but Caleb gestures with his hand, "Stop. I got this," and she backs off, begrudgingly.

Caleb stands and guides Thana's upward movement, handling her as one would an elderly person or a ventriloquist's dummy. Once standing, he allows her to find her balance before letting go. She settles into a slack, teetering posture. Her head tilts and pivots as if to take in the writhing serpent from all angles. She approaches the stage. With each dubious step, she appears to fall forward before finding her footing at the very last second.

Thana's face is on the big screen, struggling to understand… The remains of her facial musculature labors to accommodate her shifting expressions. Confusion. Reverence. Fascination. Recognition. And then… suddenly… Self-awareness.

Thana's eyes widen, the semblance of a soul behind them. Moisture where there was none before. She looks down at her hands. "Are these mine? These ARE mine…"

She lifts her head with reticent caution, like someone waking to a new reality, afraid of what they might see. Her eyes land on the writhing serpent and her focus is suddenly renewed. Her face becomes an ugly/pretty mask of sycophantic adulation. Something resembling a smile. A convulsive storm precedes arms that beckon, looking to reclaim a lost possession and never let go. She staggers forward.

Caleb is somewhere between sitting and standing, his arms held out in front of him, ready to catch Thana should she fall. His entire body spills over with hopeful anticipation. He stands and lowers his arms as she moves out of his range. He can barely contain his zeal.

116

Caleb: Thana?

Thana stops and turns. Mild recognition when she spots Caleb standing in wait, all tears and welling emotion. Thana seems intrigued by the sight of him.

Caleb smiles at her.

Caleb: It's you. Isn't it?

A sense of comfort washes over her ugly/pretty mask in response to the sound of his voice. Something resembling a smile threatens to take shape.

Movement to her right steals Thana's attention. The sight of Tina Escalante standing in the aisle inspires an immediate, visceral reaction. Thana leans closer, her head angling for a better look. Fragments of a brow wrinkle under stress.

A flash of memory enlivens Thana's frail body and turns her expression dark. A rasped groan sifts through gnashed teeth. Her eyes burn with malcontent. Without warning, Thana moves toward the center aisle and charges toward Tina. Fueled by rage, she moves with speed and fluidity uncharacteristic of her pitiful physical state. Doc Mokae takes notes in the dark background.

Tina motions for her sidearm as she backs away from the stagger-step, juggernaut. She turns a concerned look on Caleb.

Caleb: Thana! No!

Undeterred by Caleb's voice, Thana throws her arms out in front of her, her bony fingers clawing and grasping at air, telegraphing bad intentions.

Caleb: Thana!

Tina snatches a handgun from her waist and aims it at the approaching threat.

Caleb: Tina. No!

But it's too late. Fear manifests in two shots. Thana's head snaps back. She goes down hard. An ethereal trail of shattered bone and brain mist marks her quick descent.

Caleb bucks as if to an errant surge of electricity. Disbelief inhibits any further movement in the aftermath.

The music stops. The overhead screen goes black.

The boys watch from the stage. The other residents are out of their seats, reeling from a cornucopia of alarm.

Motormouth cries out "Nooo!" It takes several people to keep her from reaching for the gun hidden in her belt, her ire directed solely at Tina.

The hint of words trail off into mournful gibberish as Caleb hurries over and kneels beside the lifeless husk at Tina's feet. He lifts Thana's limp torso off the ground and cradles her in his arms. Tina stands over them, paralyzed with regret. Christian and Mateo hurry down the aisle and to her side. Doc Mokae emerges from the dark, but keeps his distance.

Tina (to Caleb): I... I had to... She was coming at me. I didn't have a choice.

His face buried in the crick of Thana's bandaged neck, Caleb rocks back and forth. He lifts her floppy, ragdoll head and mumbles sweet nothings into her partially detached ear.

Tina turns her desperation on the doctor.

Tina: I told you it wouldn't work! All you did was make her more aggressive!

Motormouth: No! It WAS her!!! It was my sister...

Motormouth struggles anew. The others work to restrain her.

Tina (to Caleb): That's not true! Don't listen to her! She's too close to this!

The others grumble in Motormouth's defense.

Caleb looks up from his dead wife, tears streaming down his swollen face.

A crackle from the overhead screen. A picture materializes…

Overhead screen

Daylight. We are part of a small group approaching a grassy embankment on the shoulder of a desolate, rural road. Christian and Mateo Escalante are in the foreground. Tina in the lead. The anonymous cameraman trailing behind them, breathing heavily. A faint, female voice pleads for help in the near-distance.

Planetarium

Tina is blindsided by the video. She lashes out at the screen like a child caught red-handed.

Tina: Turn this off!

She lifts her weapon and points it at the crowd of usual suspects on the other side of the circular row.

Tina (to usual suspects): Tell him to turn it off! Now!

Dennings steps to the front of the crowd. Mercer is right behind him.

Dennings: Not a chance!

Tina turns to her brothers.

Tina (in Spanish): Force them!

Christian and Mateo take aim at the usual suspects and

119

are met with heavily-armed defiance. Motormouth and Kovach move to the front alongside Dennings and Mercer. Kovach keeps an eye on Motormouth's dubious restraint, her handgun held in a shaky grasp.

On the stage, Graeme turns to Jules and Hollister and thrusts a questioning expression at the firearms hidden behind the drums. Jules gestures to, "Hang tight."

Caleb's head is locked in an upward tilt, his eyes glued to the screen. At this very moment, he is impervious to all distractions.

Dennings (to Escalantes): You sure about that?

Tina (re: weapons): Lying *pendejos*!

Motormouth: You're one to talk! *BITCH*!

Dennings (to Escalantes): So... What're we doing here, guys? If we all start shooting, I'm afraid you folks are gonna lose.

Realizing they are outnumbered, Tina and her brothers lower their guns. If looks could kill, Tina would be a mass murder. Motormouth, on the other hand, is much more singular in her focus.

Overhead Screen

The Escalantes and the anonymous cameraman reach the top of the embankment. A pair of tire tracks veer off the road and cut a haphazard path in the grassy area at the top of the embankment. A mid-sized creek at the bottom. An overturned car, partially submerged in dirty water. Thana Kaiser belted upside down in the driver-seat, most of her face underwater. She struggles to lift her head and hold it above water.

Crying out for help between gasps for air, she spots the group standing at the top of the embankment.

Thana: Oh! Thank God! Tina! Please help me?! I can't... I can't keep...

Thana lets her head fall beneath the water. She lifts it out a few seconds later, coughing and gasping for air.

Thana: Please hurry?! I think... the water... getting deeper...

Tina turns to the rest of the group.

Tina (re: Thana): I got this.

Tina makes her way down the embankment, turning sideways and choosing her steps with caution.

Thana: Please... hurry... Can't... breathe...

Once at the bottom, Tina casually approaches the car and crouches in front of the driver-side window. There is a brief exchange with Thana that we can't hear. Afterward, Tina stands and uses her foot to push Thana's face underneath the water. She puts up a futile struggle, but Tina holds her foot there until Thana stops moving.

A gasp from the anonymous cameraman.

Tina looks up at the group standing at the top of the embankment.

Tina: The bitch was dead when we found her!

Static... The screen goes black...

Planetarium

Anxiety spreads throughout the room. Nervous speculation from the onlookers awaiting Caleb's reaction. After several minutes of inactivity, his head begins a slow descent from the overhead screen. He face is bloated from crying, yet otherwise absent of any discernable emotion. His eyes skim the woman standing in front of him, radiating guilt. She reaches out to him…

Tina (to Caleb): I can explain…

Caleb silences her with a raised hand. Afterward, he lays his dead wife on the floor and gently strokes the brittle wisps of degraded, strawberry-blond hair stuck to her rotted scalp. Without looking away, he calmly addresses the armed crowd of usual suspects.

Caleb: Lower your guns.

Apprehension from the armed crowd, save for Motormouth, whose expression speaks for her, "Fuck that!"

The others look to Dennings for direction. At the moment, he has none to give.

Caleb: I know you're all worried that I'm not in control of my own faculties… and that I haven't been for some time. Well… Let me assure you. As of this very moment, my head has never been clearer. Now. Lower… your… weapons…

Dennings returns a look meant to spot-evaluate Caleb's mindset. He lowers his weapon seconds later. Motormouth stands firm. The others follow Dennings' lead and lower their weapons.

Dennings lays a hand on Motormouth's wrist, whispers something in her ear, and then guides her arm downward. Her vengeance unrequited, she starts to weep. Kovach slides an arm around her shoulders and pulls her close.

Tina (to Caleb): I know you're angry with me. But please, just listen… You know my story… My loss… My husband… My little Perdita… How I was ready to give up… to throw in the towel until I met you. You gave me something to live for…

Motormouth: NO! YOU DON'T GET TO HAVE A SOB STORY!

Kovach grabs Motormouth by the shoulders and turns her around. He takes her face in both hands, leans in so close that the tips of their noses touch, and quietly appeals to her patience.

Tina continues, undeterred by the outburst.

Tina (to Caleb): I... I was so afraid of losing you that I must have just panicked... I'm so sorry.

Caleb stares through Tina with dead eyes and the face of a spirit crushed, and stomped on, and turned to apathy as a means of defense. He puts his feet underneath him and stands, nodding as if having reached some level of acceptance.

Caleb gives no indication of his next move, exploding into action with liquid efficiency. By the end of it, Christian and Mateo Escalante lay on their backs, face-up to the darkened screen. A single bullet-hole placed dead-center in each of their foreheads.

Caleb drops his arm to his side. His eyes track up, from the bodies on the floor, and stop on Tina. She appears less affected by the result of the gunshots than by the sound they made, which had startled everyone within earshot.

Caleb (to Tina, re: her brothers): I don't know what happened... I guess I just panicked.

Tina gives her dead brothers a quick glance and then returns her attention to Caleb as if they are no more than a pair of squashed insects.

Tina: It's okay. As long as I still have you.

The remark reaches through Caleb's unaffected exterior.

Caleb (incredulous): Who, the Hell, are you?!

Tina: I'm the woman you love. Remember?

Caleb: SHUT UP! JUST SHUT! UP!

Tina looks at the ground.

Following a prelude of silent introspection and measured breathing, Caleb turns to the usual suspects and looks on them with affection.

Equal affection in return...

Caleb: You were right to worry about me. I'm afraid I haven't been myself lately. I acted out of weakness, desperation... and you've all suffered as a result. For that I am deeply sorry. Thanks to your persistence, I see it now. (glances at Tina) And I hear what you've been trying to tell me all along.

Caleb points his gun at Tina. She winces, turns her head away, and hides behind her hands.

Tina: Please don't?! I love you!

Caleb (to Tina): You're good. I'll give you that. For awhile there, you had my head screwed up somethin' awful. But I see you now. I *SEE* you... I see the monster behind that pretty face and all that fancy psychobabble. And I know now what you really are; a heartless, gutless, spineless *bitch,* who'd kill her mother to save her own ass.

Tina: No! That's not true!

Caleb: Tell me something? Your husband... Your little Perdita... D'ju kill them, too?

Tina starts to cry.

Tina: How can you say that to me?

Caleb rolls his eyes.

Caleb: Either way, it ends here. Because I'm going to take from you the one thing that you value most.

124

Tina shrinks as Caleb tightens his grip around the handle of the gun and refocuses his aim at her head.

Tina: Caleb! No!

Caleb hesitates. The crowd waits in breathless anticipation, a satisfied sneer plastered across Motormouth's face.

Caleb lowers his arm to the disappointment of the usual suspects. A glint of relief brings Tina out from behind her hands. A meek smile takes shape.

Caleb pulls the trigger. The bullet punches through Tina's abdomen and folds her like a lawn chair. Her eyes nearly burst from their sockets. She makes a strange sound, like a rush of air forced out at the onset of a baritone grunt, and slaps her hands over her belly. Her knees buckle. She stumbles over Mateo's body, hits the ground in a tight ball, and rolls around on the floor, bleeding out, her painful cries like some wailing ballad performed by a tone-deaf R & B Diva.

Seeming to take no satisfaction from his deed, Caleb drops his arm to his side. His eyes find Doc Mokae standing at the mouth of the dark background, taking it all in with clinical curiosity.

Caleb (to Doc Mokae, re: Tina): That fresh specimen you always wanted... Give her a few hours and she's yours. Call it a gift.

Tina groans in protest between coughing fits.

Caleb (to Tina): I suggest you take that time to contemplate the end of your existence. And while you're at it, you can think about all the fun the doctor is going to have with you when you wake up dead. I want you to *feel* the *pain* you caused my Thana... The *pain* you caused our family here at Great Plains. And I want you to understand that there's not a *damn thing* you can do about it.

Tina: How… can you… do this to me?

Caleb shakes his head in disgust and then turns to his extended family.

Caleb: Somebody get her outta my sight.

Motormouth springs forward like she had been poised on starting blocks.

Caleb thrusts an open hand at her.

Caleb (to Motormouth): No!

Motormouth stops and casts an annoyed glare at Caleb.

Caleb: I'm sorry, Starr, but the idea is for her to appreciate everything she's about to lose. I let you take her and I doubt she'd even make it to the infirmary, let alone make it there alive. Mercer and Kovach can take her.

Motormouth looks on Tina with contempt. In her mind she murders her several times over.

Kovach gives Motormouth a pat on the shoulder as he and Mercer hurry past. They grab Tina under the armpits, drag her up the aisle, kicking, and screaming, and coughing up blood, and out through the Corridor C doors. Motormouth watches them like a dog waiting patiently for a tasty morsel to fall from the dinner table.

Tina wails in absentia, her voice shrinking in volume as the Corridor C doors swing closed. The click of the latch precedes an eerie silence.

Caleb kneels over Thana's crumpled husk and takes her in his arms. He holds her close, kisses her on the forehead, and begins stroking her hair.

Caleb (to Thana): I'm so sorry, baby. This is all my doing. I broke my vows as a husband and set this whole awful thing in motion. There's really nothing I can say that will make up for the pain I've caused you...

He looks up, finds Motormouth, the doctor, and the rest of his extended family.

Caleb: ...that I've caused all of you.

Grumbles of disapproval from the onlookers.

Caleb: It's okay. I can accept it now. Just like I accept that I am no longer fit to be your leader.

Motormouth: You *are* our leader. Why, the Hell, d'ju think we fought so hard to get you back?

Caleb shakes his head, "No."

Caleb: That's sweet. And I love you all for it. But, I'm not the man I used to be. You know it's true.

No one responds.

Caleb: Dennings is a good man. He'll make a fine leader.

Motormouth: What are *you* gonna do?

Caleb looks down at his wife.

Caleb: My place is with Thana. There's nothing left for me here.

Sensing Caleb's next move, Motormouth motions toward him with sudden urgency, but Caleb is too swift and efficient in his action, placing his gun against his right temple and pulling the trigger.

Motormouth gasps into her hands, and turns away. The rest of the family reacts similarly. A few of them brave the awful sight as Caleb's head jerks violently to the left, spurting bloody brain-matter from the newly bored exit-wound just above his ear. His body goes limp beneath him and he crumbles to the floor.

Her hands held over her mouth, Motormouth approaches Caleb's body. Standing over him, she breaks down in tears once again. A few of the others make their way toward her.

"Beck's Bolero," by The Jeff Beck Group starts to play over the scene.

Jules (V.O.): Love is a crazy thing, man. You'd think after watching something like that I'd want nothing to do with it, but the fact is, I kinda envied the poor bastard. Having that kind of connection with a good woman ain't nothin' to laugh at. All the pussy in the world can't hold a candle to it. And that's coming from someone who's had his fair share.

Video (Great Plains CCTV Cam)

Cemetery

"Beck's Bolero" continues to play.

White picket fencing wraps around a cemetery built into the backyard of the Great Plains' Haunted House. A crowd of solemn faces stand at the foot of two freshly covered graves laid-out side-by-side and marked by crosses fashioned from cut wood. "Caleb Kaiser" and "Thana Moon Kaiser" scrawled in marker on the face of each cross. More crosses mark the graves of previously deceased family members. A barrier of souvenir and food kiosks just beyond the white picket fencing conceals the proceedings from the dead gathered at the gates. The peaks and valleys of the Sidewinder Rollercoaster loom, like some giant skeletal sea-serpent, in the background.

Jules, Graeme, and Hollister stand at the front of the crowd. Jules, with his eyes squeezed shut, gently fingers an acoustic guitar strapped across his torso.

Jules (V.O.): It only made sense that we play them out...

128

Their story was like a song I had yet to write. Hell. I could probably devote an entire album to it. I kept picturing them together somewhere laughing at us suckers fighting tooth-n-nail to stay alive.

Video (Canon Vixia HF HD Cam – Graeme's POV)

"Route 66," by The Cramps plays over the scene.

The tricked out Ford Sportsmobile sits idle a few yards inside the main entrance archway. On the other side, a wall of truck trailers line the fence that extends to the left and right of the archway as far as the eye can see. The damaged trailer has been replaced. An anonymous Great Plains resident sits behind the wheel of the trailer parked directly in front of the archway, waiting for the word to start the engine and move the vehicle. Several armed residents move back and forth atop neighboring trailers, surveying the area on the other side.

Dennings, Mercer, Kovach, and Motormouth head a small group gathered outside the van as the boys load up with supplies between handshakes and hugs. Graeme operating the Vixia.

Jules (V.O.): It felt good to leave a place on good terms for a change. They thanked us for setting things straight, gave us food and ammo for the short drive to the Weather, and a warning from Dennings to steer clear of the Suitland Parkway area. They had heard over the radio that Swarm's prized hostage had escaped, which meant that...

A. They're currently out looking for him/her.
B. They're looking for another hostage of note to replace him/her.

Dennings suggested a round-about route to get there. "It'll tack another hour onto your drive. But at least you'll get there in one piece," he goes. Duly noted.

Mads Angle gave us all the CCTV Camera footage from our

visit. "Make sure you spell my name right in the credits," he goes. "And tell 'em I'm available if they're hirin'."

Mads-fucking-Angle, ladies and gentleman...

The boys climb into the van as Dennings and Kovach walk up to the main gate. Graeme attaches the Vixia to the dashboard mount and points it out the windshield.

Dennings communicates via walkie-talkie with the residents atop the trailers. They line up along the length of the trailers and aim their weapons toward the ground. One of them gives Dennings a thumbs up. The resident behind the wheel of the trailer starts the engine.

Dennings and Kovach work together to open the gate. The group waves the boys off as they drive through.

Video (Canon Vixia HF HD Cam)

"Route 66," continues to play...

...an aquamarine sky, cloudless and punctuated by a brilliant ball of heat. No sign of movement until the camera tilts down to the rotoscope blur of tree-tops, and billboards, and water towers, indicative of a vehicle traveling a moderate speed on an idyllic spring day. A rolling tour of ghost towns and toxic landscapes interrupted by pockets of recovery. Upright corpses lumber directionless on the sidelines. They stop to discern the passing vehicle as food or foe, like curious beasts on safari. Some seek shelter. The van swerves to avoid the occasional obstacle.

Interior of van

Plush, leather seating. All black. Tinted windows. The illusion of space in back. Leather bench and console. Boxes and guitar cases stacked against the rear doors. Idyllic scenery peeking in through the windows.

Jules is seated on the bench in back, a face full of optimism pointed out the window. Acoustic guitar laid on next to him. Hollister and Graeme in the driver and passenger-seats, respectively. The windows are down.

Jules (V.O.): There's something magical about the road, even in a world where dead people come back to life, ESP-induced apparitions are a real thing, and the living have gone all "Every man... and woman... for his or her self." Maybe it was the forward motion; moving on toward our final destination, and all that. Maybe it was doing it in the company of good friends. Or maybe it was just that it was nice to feel the sun's warmth again on such a beautiful fucking day.

An undead man wandering on the road-shoulder, up ahead. He turns toward the van as they approach. His face is a skinless mask dried out over time, all bug-eyes and skeletal grimace embedded in a slow-moving mural of subcutaneous calamity.

Jules (V.O.): Even the deadfucks are smiling.

Greame leans out the passenger-side window and waves to the smiling dead man.

Graeme (to smiling dead man): Beautiful day. Huh?!

Suddenly...

A record scratch. The music stops. The van slows down.

The van slowly approaches a man-made roadblock of stacked vehicles. No way around it.

Jules (re: roadblock): Son-of-a-bitch!

Interior of van / Scenery outside windows - later

The music has been replaced by the engine's smooth, perpetual groan, and by the mesmerizing hum of rubber against road. There is no other sound.

131

Jules is seated on the bench in back, his hands resting on an automatic weapon lying across his lap. A concerned expression pointed out the window. Hollister and Graeme in the driver and passenger-seats, respectively. Both are armed and hyper-focused on the obstacle course that is the Suitland Parkway. Wooded walls hug the road on both sides, "Swarm" crudely spray-painted over every mile-marker and Suitland Parkway sign they pass.

Jules (V.O.): There's something about the road that makes me want to get right, the fuck, off of it. Give me the predictable monotony of a good settlement over this endless fucking cock-block. I'm too old for it anymore. We all are. Eighty miles 'til the Promised Land and our place at the table is under threat by a bunch fucknuts lookin' to possibly ambush us for ransom. No way we were gonna let that happen. No fucking way…

It was so quiet that I could hear myself think after awhile. Holly must've been listening. He reached for the radio and turned on the Martin Stone Show just as the thought popped into my head.

Raven's voice doesn't pack the same medicinal punch when you're actively worried about that bullet, blade, or blunt instrument… or teeth, for that matter, with your name on it, finally finding you. The edge came off in layers as I half-listened. It was the ass-end of a survivor-story; some dude who got himself cornered in an outhouse surrounded by dead-fucks and had to crawl down into the pit and tunnel his way out using a garden-trowel. Poor bastard survived the whole thing only to be hit with a raging case of Hepatitis B. Talk about shit luck.

A promo for our arrival leads into a commercial break… Raven mentions how stoked Martin would be to have a band of our caliber representing the show, and I just about got a woody.

On the road-shoulder, a frail, human-shape darts out from behind an overturned minivan and crosses the Sportsmobile's path, with less than five feet to spare. It appears to be a man, long and tall, dressed in tatters, with a tangled mane of curly black hair whipping in tow. Hollister slams on the brakes. The van slides toward the lanky blur, tires squealing as if reacting to an imminent collision. Another figure darts out in pursuit of the first. He looks healthier by comparison. Well-feed. Well-armed. Better clothing, which consists of a T-shirt and desert-camo cargo pants. A tattoo of an "S" stands out against the pale skin of his forearm.

The pursuer is on the first man's tail. His focus is so singular that it sedates his other senses, like the one that should have warned him about the bulky, black Ford that would surely kill him if he ran out from behind that overturned minivan.

Acknowledgement comes seconds before impact, as the pursuer turns and blasts the reluctant spectators on the other side of the windshield with a horrified shock-face.

Hollister grips the steering wheel and squeezes his eyes shut. Jules and Graeme look away.

The pursuer throws his arms up in a futile defensive effort. The grille-guard pulverizes his limbs, pinning the shattered remains to his chest, which then collapses beneath the forward thrust of 8500 pounds. A thick spray of bloody vomitus coats the windshield. The pursuer's head flops, snapping his neck. His face smacks the hood like a furious kowtow. Some of the details remain embedded in the hood as his head bounces back and the concussive force launches his limp carcass into the air.

The van stops. Raven's voice on the radio is the only sound. The boys unfurl from tight poses like flowers in bloom. Hollister flips a switch on the steering column and watches with reluctance as the windshield wipers smear the blood enough for them to see through.

The pursuer lie in a pile of limbs and exposed viscera, 30-feet away, nearly indecipherable as human. A crimson trail marks his shambolic slide to rest.

Inside the van, no one speaks. Hollister reaches for the door handle…

Jules: Wait!

Hollister stops. His response is interrupted by a rain of bullets against the right side of the van. The boys jump, grab their weapons. Graeme leans away from the bullet-proof glass.

Jules: SHIT! LET'S GET THE FUCK OUTTA HERE!

Graeme: DRIVE! DRIVE! DRIVE!

Hollister throws the van into drive and…

A pounding on the driver-side door. Hollister slides away from the sound, grabs his gun, and aims it at the long, tall shape on the other side of the window. It's a man, the same one the pursuer had been chasing. He looks disheveled, malnourished, and mentally broken, standing there shivering and out of breath, his arms raised in surrender. Something immediately familiar about him, but the details of his dirt-smudged face are concealed behind shoulder-length black hair matted with sweat. His voice is barely more than a rasp.

Disheveled man: You've gotta help me! They're after me! I'll die before I let them take me back to that place!

Hollister leans away from the terrified man, and then it hits him.

Hollister: Holy shit! Martin Stone?!

Dedicated to the music of...

Jimi Hendrix, Led Zeppelin, The Rolling Stones, AC/DC, Iron Butterfly, Guns N Roses, Metallica, The Clash, The Cramps, The Cult, Cheap Trick, Rush, Sugarloaf, Quiet Riot, KISS, Twisted Sister, Goblin, Dick Dale, Ozzy Osborne, Alice Cooper, Billy Idol, Van Halen, Queensryche, Motley Crue, Bon Jovi, Aerosmith, Def Leppard, Poison, RATT, Tesla, Scorpions, Skid Row, Slaughter, Warrant, Cinderella, Whitesnake, Winger, Great White, L.A. Guns, Lita Ford, early Heart, Joan Jett, Serpentine

For those about to rock...
- AC/DC

Andre Duza is an actor, stuntman, screenwriter, and the author or co-author of over 10 novels, a graphic novel, Hollow-Eyed Mary, and the Star Trek comic book Outer Light, co-written with writer/producer Morgan Gendel. He has also contributed to several collections and anthologies, including Book of Lists: Horror, alongside the likes of Stephen King and Eli Roth.

Andre's distinctive blend of cult-horror, science-fiction, and dark comedy has been described as weird, off-beat, intense, horrific, satirical, and fast-paced, with a unique voice and lush, finely-detailed prose.

Andre also wrote, co-produced, and starred in the award-winning short film Tagati, which is currently making the rounds on the festival circuit. You can view the trailer on YouTube here: https://www.youtube.com/watch?v=uUZ6na3TBxI

"Header" Edward Lee - In the dark backwoods, where law enforcement doesn't dare tread, there exists a special type of revenge. Something so awful that it is only whispered about. Something so terrible that few believe it is real. Stewart Cummings is a government agent whose life is going to Hell. His wife is ill and to pay for her medication he turns to bootlegging. But things will get much worse when bodies begin showing up in his sleepy small town. Victims of an act known only as "a Header."

"Punk Rock Ghost Story" David Agranoff - In the summer of 1982, legendary Indianapolis hardcore band, The Fuckers, became the victim of a mysterious tragedy. They returned home without their vocalist and the band disappeared. A single record sought by collectors, a band nearly forgotten, and an urban legend passed from punk to punk. What happened to The Fuckers on that tour? Why was their singer never seen again? No one has been able to say. Until now…

"Zombies and Shit" Carlton Mellick III - Twenty people wake to find themselves in a boarded-up building in the middle of the zombie wasteland. They soon discover they have been chosen as contestants on a popular reality show called Zombie Survival. Each contestant is given a backpack of supplies and a unique weapon. Their goal: be the first to make it through the zombie-plagued city to the pick-up zone alive. But because there's only one seat available on the helicopter, the contestants not only have to fight against the hordes of the living dead, they must also fight each other.

"The Book of a Thousand Sins" Wrath James White - Welcome to a world of Zombie nymphomaniacs, psychopathic deities, voodoo surgery, and murderous priests. Where mutilation sex clubs are in vogue and torture machines are sex toys. No one makes it out alive – not even God himself.
"If Wrath James White doesn't make you cringe, you must be riding in the wrong end of a hearse."
  -Jack Ketchum

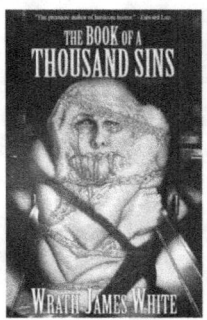

"Like Porno for Psychos" Wrath James White - From a world-ending orgy to home liposuction. From the hidden desires of politicians to a woman with a fetish for lions. This is a place where necrophilia, self-mutilation, and murder are all roads to love. Like Porno for Psychos collects the most extreme erotic horror from the celebrated hardcore horror master. Wrath James White is your guide through sex, death, and the darkest desires of the heart.

"Bigfoot Crank Stomp" Erik Williams - Bigfoot is real and he's addicted to meth! It should have been so easy. Get in, kill everyone, and take all the money and drugs. That was Russell and Mickey's plan. But the drug den they were raiding in the middle of the woods holds a dark secret chained up in the basement. A beast filled with rage and methamphetamine and tonight it will break loose. Nothing can stop Bigfoot's drug-fueled rampage and before the sun rises there is going to be a lot of dead cops and junkies.

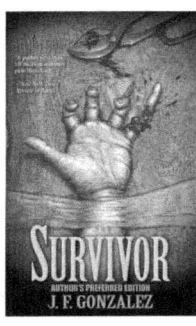

"Survivor" J.F. Gonzalez - Lisa was looking forward to spending time alone with her husband. Instead, it becomes a nightmare when her husband is arrested and Lisa is kidnapped. But the kidnappers aren't asking for ransom. They're going to make her a star-in a snuff film.. They plan to torture and murder her as graphically and brutally as possible, and to capture it all on film. If they have their way, Lisa's death will be truly horrifying...but even more horrifying is what Lisa will do to survive...

"Genital Grinder" Ryan Harding - *"Think you're hardcore? Think again. If you've handled everything Edward Lee, Wrath James White, and Bryan Smith have thrown at you, then put on your rubber parka, spread some plastic across the floor, and get ready for Ryan Harding, the unsung master of hardcore horror. Abandon all hope, ye who enter here. Harding's work is like an acid bath, and pain has never been so sweet."*
- Brian Keene

AVAILABLE FROM AMAZON.COM

deadite press

"WZMB" Andre Duza - It's the end of the world, but we're not going off the air! Martin Stone was a popular shock jock radio host before the zombie apocalypse. Then for six months the dead destroyed society. Humanity is now slowly rebuilding and Martin Stone is back to doing what he does best-taking to the airwaves. Host of the only radio show in this new world, he helps organize other survivors. But zombies aren't the only threat. There are others that thought humanity needed to end.

"Tribesmen" Adam Cesare - Thirty years ago, cynical sleazeball director Tito Bronze took a tiny cast and crew to a desolate island. His goal: to exploit the local tribes, spray some guts around, cash in on the gore-spattered 80s Italian cannibal craze. But the pissed-off spirits of the island had other ideas. And before long, guts were squirting behind the scenes, as well. While the camera kept rolling...

"Reincarnage" Ryan Harding and Jason Taverner - In the 80's a supernatural killer known as Agent Orange terrorized the United States. No matter how many times he was killed, he kept coming back to spread death and mayhem. With no other choice, the government walled off the small town, woods, and lake that Agent Orange used as his hunting ground. This seemed to contain the killer and his killing sprees ended. Or so the populace thought...

"Suffer the Flesh" Monica J. O'Rourke - Zoey always wished she was thinner. One day she meets a strange woman who informs her of an ultimate weight-loss program, and Zoey is quickly abducted off the streets of Manhattan and forced into this program. Zoey's enrolling whether she wants to or not. Held hostage with many other women, Zoey is forced into degrading acts of perversion for the amusement of her captors. ...

"Answers of Silence" Geoff Cooper - Deadite Press is proud to present the extremely sought after horror stories of Geoff Cooper. Collecting fifteen tales of the weird, the horrific, and the strange. Fans of Brian Keene, Jack Ketchum, and Bryan Smith won't want to miss this collection from one of the unsung masters of modern horror. You won't forget your visit to Geoff Cooper's dark and deranged world.

"Boot Boys of the Wolf Reich" David Agranoff - PIt is the summer of 1989 and they spend their days hanging out and having fun, and their nights fighting the local neo-Nazi gangs. Driven back and badly beaten, the local Nazi contingent finds the strangest of allies - The last survivor of a cult of Nazi werewolf assassins. An army of neo-Nazi werewolves are just what he needs. But first, they have some payback for all those meddling Anti-racist SHARPs...

"White Trash Gothic" Edward Lee - Luntville is not just some bumfuck town in the sticks. It is a place where the locals make extra cash by filming necro porn, a place where vigilantes practice a horrifying form of justice they call deaddickin', a place haunted by the ghosts of serial killers, occult demons, and a monster called the Bighead. And as the writer attempts to make sense of the town and his connection to it, he will be challenged in ways that test the very limit of his sanity.

"Whargoul" Dave Brockie - It is a beast born in bullets and shrapnel, feeding off of pain, misery, and hard drugs. Cursed to wander the Earth without the hope of death, it is reborn again and again to spread the gospel of hate, abuse, and genocide. But what if it's not the only monster out there? What if there's something worse? From Dave Brockie, the twisted genius behind GWAR, comes a novel about the darkest days of the twentieth century.

AVAILABLE FROM AMAZON.COM

deadite press

"Brain Cheese Buffet" Edward Lee - collecting nine of Lee's most sought after tales of violence and body fluids. Featuring the Stoker nominated "Mr. Torso," the legendary gross-out piece "The Dritiphilist," the notorious "The McCrath Model SS40-C, Series S," and six more stories to test your gag reflex.
"Edward Lee's writing is fast and mean as a chain saw revved to full-tilt boogie."
    - Jack Ketchum

"Ghoul" Brian Keene - There is something in the local cemetery that comes out at night. Something that is unearthing corpses and killing people. It's the summer of 1984 and Timmy and his friends are looking forward to no school, comic books, and adventure. But instead they will be fighting for their lives. The ghoul has smelled their blood and it is after them. But that's not the only monster they will face this summer . . . From award-winning horror master Brian Keene comes a novel of monsters, murder, and the loss of innocence.

"The Dark Ones" Bryan Smith - They are The Dark Ones. The name began as a self-deprecating joke, but it stuck and now it's a source of pride. They're the one who don't fit in. The misfits who drink and smoke too much and stay out all hours of the night. Everyone knows they're trouble. On the outskirts of Ransom, TN is an abandoned, boarded-up house. Something evil happened there long ago. The evil has been contained there ever since, locked down tight in the basement—until the night The Dark Ones set it free . . .

"His Pain" Wrath James White - Life is pain . . . . . . or at least it is for Jason. Born with a rare central nervous disorder, every sensation is pain. Every sound, scent, texture, flavor, even every breath, brings nothing but mind-numbing pain. Until the arrival of Yogi Arjunda of the Temple of Physical Enlightenment. He claims to be able to help Jason, to be able to give him a life of more than agony. But the treatment leaves Jason changed and he wants to share what he learned. He wants to share his pain . . . A novella of pain, pleasure, and transcendental splatter.

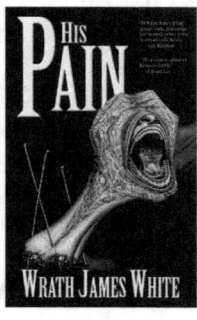

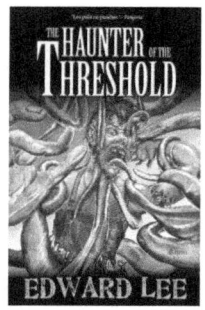

"The Haunter of the Threshold" Edward Lee - There is something very wrong with this backwater town. Suicide notes, magic gems, and haunted cabins await her. Plus the woods are filled with monsters, both human and otherworldly. And then there are the horrible tentacles . . . Soon Hazel is thrown into a battle for her life that will test her sanity and sex drive. The sequel to H.P. Lovecraft's The Haunter of the Dark is Edward Lee's most pornographic novel to date!

"Baby's First Book of Seriously Fucked-Up Shit" Robert Devereaux - From an orgy between God, Satan, Adam and Eve to beauty pageants for fetuses. From a giant human-absorbing tongue to a place where God is in the eyes of the psychopathic. This is a party at the furthest limits of human decency and cruelty. Robert Devereaux is your host but watch out, he's spiked the punch with drugs, sex, and dismemberment. Deadite Press is proud to present nine stories of the strange, the gross, and the just plain fucked up.

"Highways to Hell" Bryan Smith - The road to hell is paved with angels and demons. Brain worms and dead prostitutes. Serial killers and frustrated writers. Zombies and Rock 'n Roll. And once you start down this path, there is no going back. Collecting thirteen tales of shock and terror from Bryan Smith, Highways to Hell is a non-stop road-trip of cruelty, pain, and death. Grab a seat, Smith has such sights to show you.

"Apeshit" Carlton Mellick III - Friday the 13th meets Visitor Q. Six hipster teens go to a cabin in the woods inhabited by a deformed killer. An incredibly fucked-up parody of B-horror movies with a bizarro slant

"The new gold standard in unstoppable fetus-fucking kill-freakomania . . . Genuine all-meat hardcore horror meets unadulterated Bizarro brainwarp strangeness. The results are beyond jaw-dropping, and fill me with pure, unforgivable joy." - John Skipp

AVAILABLE FROM AMAZON.COM

www.ingramcontent.com/pod-product-compliance
Lightning Source LLC
Chambersburg PA
CBHW060425260626
47161CB00005B/1782